CLOSE QUARTERS

BROKEN BOW

BOOK FOUR

ASHLEY A QUINN

TCA PUBLISHING LLC

Author's Note

The use of CRISPR technology to facilitate DNA sequencing in forensics is not new, but it is still cutting-edge science. Normal DNA sequencing requires amplification of the short tandem repeat (STR) sections of human DNA used in forensic science. In other words, the DNA must be copied many times over to get an adequate size for the test to work. In the 2010s, scientists began using the CRISPR technique to analyze these STR sections without the amplification process, allowing forensic scientists to use more degraded samples and get accurate results.

Why am I telling you this? Because the spunky Katie Mitchum starring in this novel is in the process of obtaining her Ph.D. using this technique. It is actual science, and I wanted to give some background on the research. I didn't make it all up, I swear!

Happy reading!
~Ashley

ONE

"Oh, come on!" Dr. Alex Randall looked around his pathology lab, his anger growing as he took in the mess that bloomed overnight.

Katie Mitchum, the county's chief forensic scientist, poked her head up from behind a large boxy machine, her pink-framed glasses sliding down her nose and tendrils of her colorful hair fluttering around her pretty face.

"Seriously, Katie? Where the hell did all this shit come from? I have to work down here, too, you know." He tossed his briefcase down onto the autopsy table and put his hands on his hips, glaring at her.

She rolled her hazel eyes. "Take a chill pill, Doc. Once I get it organized, it won't look as bad."

He looked around the room, which was already stuffed to the gills. "Where are you going to put it that will make it look better?"

Her eyes followed the track his took, and she shrugged. "Somewhere. I just need to shift a couple things. What are you complaining about, anyway? You don't even use all the space down here."

He pinched the bridge of his nose, a headache already forming. "I did before you showed up."

The look she leveled on him said she thought he'd grown another head. "Sure you did. That's why it was so easy for me to move in."

Alex scrubbed his hands over his face. He couldn't wait for the county to rebuild the criminology lab so he could get her out of his space. She was driving him crazy. "Okay. Sure. I don't want to argue. Can you please just—" he motioned around the room with his hands, "move things so we have more space to work? I feel like I'm tripping over everything."

She scrunched her nose and frowned, but nodded.

"Thank you." Picking up his briefcase, he walked past her toward his office on the far side of the large room. At least she hadn't invaded it too. He put his key in the lock and opened the door. Flipping on the light, he groaned. Three more filing cabinets lined the walls.

"How the hell did she even get in here?" he muttered.

"Oh, I meant to text you about those last night, and I forgot," Katie said from behind him. He turned to look at her. "They delivered the new evidence dryer and gas chromatograph. I needed space, so I asked security to unlock your office."

His jaw worked as he looked down at her. "I thought we agreed my office was off-limits?"

She shrugged. "I needed the space."

"Find space somewhere else."

"It's just a couple filing cabinets, Alex."

"Don't care. Stay out of my office. You have until the end of the day, or they're going out in the hallway."

She sighed and adjusted her glasses. "Fine, sourpuss." Rolling her eyes once more, she turned and sauntered away.

Alex grabbed the edge of the door and flung it closed. That woman was going to be the death of him. If he thought he could find a better forensic scientist, he'd fire her ass for insubordination. Her skill was the only thing keeping her employed.

He blew out a breath and shrugged out of his coat. Truthfully, she wasn't that bad. She irritated him, yes, but she was kind and funny and the best damn forensic tech he'd ever worked with. There were just some days where her tendency to take charge ground on his last nerve. Which had been much more frequent since she moved into his lab.

Hanging his jacket on the back of his chair, he sat down to filter through his email. The phone rang, and he reached for it while he continued to skim through his inbox. "Dr. Randall."

"Hey, Alex, it's Seb."

Alex focused on the conversation at the sound of the sheriff's voice coming over the line. "Hey, Seb. What's up?"

"How fast can you put together a team to scour the Paulsons' mountain property?"

He frowned. "The place where they held all those kids captive?"

"That's the one. After I got a full statement from Mason and from the kids we rescued, not to mention all the information Anne readily gave up on her husband and Judge Brandt, I have reason to believe there are several bodies buried up there. Judge Kovac signed off on my warrant first thing this morning."

"We can probably get out there tomorrow morning if we prep today. Do you have a cadaver dog? I'm not sure if Katie has a radar unit. If she doesn't, we might have to contact Denver or Colorado Springs for assistance."

"I haven't looked into K-9 assistance yet, but I will. I might be able to get a dog from the state. Why don't you find out about the radar unit, and we'll go from there?"

"Will do. I have a question, though. When you say several,

do you have a more specific number?" He wanted to make sure they had enough supplies on hand.

"Best guess, at least four. The kids came at different times, with Mason there the longest. But he said there was at least one who was there before him and disappeared while he was held captive. He said he remembers two others as well who vanished. Anne claims Jim handled most of the dealings with their clientele. She says she was just there to help kidnap the kids and keep them clothed and fed."

"Do you believe her?"

"Maybe. When I talked to her, she was in the midst of detox for heroin, so she was a twitchy mess. I'm not sure she remembers much of what went on in that house with any clarity. When I asked her specifically about any of the kids disappearing before they kidnapped Mason, she said there were a couple, but couldn't give me a specific number. I figure you're looking for four to seven, maybe eight, bodies. I tried to get Jim and the judge to give me details, but they refused to say anything."

"Jesus. That's disgusting."

"Tell me about it." Seb's voice was terse. "I can't wait for this case to go to trial. I'm going to pin every charge I can think of on all three of them."

"Okay. Let me talk to my team and I'll get back to you."

"Sounds good."

Alex hung up and sighed. He had no idea where he was going to put that many bodies with only a quarter of a lab. He glanced at the filing cabinets against the wall. Maybe a quarter was too generous.

Pushing away from his desk, he stood and exited his office. More of Katie's team had arrived, and they were busy moving things around to improve the flow of the room. He spotted his quarry, bent over a lab table, trying to reach the outlet behind it. Alex tried not to stare as he got a full view of her tight butt in her khaki jeans. Katie Mitchum might annoy the ever-loving shit out of him most of the time, but she was a knockout.

He walked over to her and cleared his throat. She glanced up at him.

"What now? Look, I'm trying to make some more space, okay?" She straightened, still holding the power cord.

"It's not about that. Seb just called. We need to prep for an excavation."

Her brow dipped with curiosity. "Okay, which cemetery?"

"Not a cemetery. The Paulsons' place."

"The human traffickers?"

He nodded. "Apparently, there are several children buried up there."

A dark frown overtook her face. "I can't believe Judge Brandt masterminded that whole thing. I hope he fries. When do we need to be ready?"

"Tomorrow, if possible."

She bit her lip and looked around. "I'm not sure that's doable, to be honest. I need to borrow a radar. Mine's on order still."

"Okay. What else do you need that you don't have?"

"That's it. Everything else I'd need for a body recovery I've already replaced."

He nodded. "Sounds good. Get enough supplies and personnel lined up for at least eight bodies. That's the high end, but we don't want to be short on what we need once we get out there. I'm going to make some calls and see about finding you that radar. I need to talk to Amanda Pressley at the University of Colorado too. I think all our remains are going to be skeletonized, and I don't deal with just bones."

"Will do, boss." Her mouth quirked as she gave him a sharp salute.

He rolled his eyes and plucked the cord from her fingers,

leaning over the table to plug it in. "Get busy," he said, straightening. Spinning on his heel, he went back to his office.

Exhausted, Katie fell into the chair at her desk and closed her eyes. It was eight p.m., and she'd been at work since seven that morning. Alex had come through with the radar and the forensic anthropologist. Both were meeting them at the Paulsons' tomorrow morning, so she and her team had launched into overdrive to get things ready.

Her stomach growled, reminding her she skipped dinner, and that lunch was the protein bar she kept in her desk. But she didn't want to move. Her feet hurt and so did her back. She was only thirty-two, but right now, she felt more like she was sixty-two.

The soft snick of a door opening made her open her eyes. She swiveled to watch Alex step out of his office. Dark stubble dusted his jawline, and his chocolate hair with its hint of silver was mussed. She bit her lip as she watched him walk. Even rumpled, the man was a sight to behold. At a couple inches over six feet, the medical examiner's muscled frame moved with a predatory grace. Intelligence sparked out of his bright blue eyes, and she knew if he smiled, they would crinkle at the corners. She'd never had a thing for older men until she met Alex Randall.

Although he wasn't *that* much older than she was. When he started working for the county, she peeked at his personnel file, more than a little curious about the handsome doctor, and discovered he had eleven years on her.

Her chair creaked as she shifted while she watched him walk to the door. He paused and glanced back.

"What are you still doing here? I thought everyone was gone except for the handful of night shift employees."

She sat up and rolled to the drawers that made up one side of her desk, removing her purse. "They are. I stayed to finish a few things. But it's time for me to leave now, too." She picked up her coat and shrugged into it.

"I'll walk you out."

"You don't have to do that. I'll be fine." She really didn't want to walk all the way to the employee parking lot with him. Part of the reason she antagonized him so much was to keep him at arm's length. He did funny things to her insides whenever he got too close. Or smiled.

"I don't mind. We're going the same way, anyway."

She searched her brain for a reason to walk alone, but anything she came up with was lame; he'd see right through her for the chicken she was.

"Fine. But don't blame me when you get annoyed by the sound of my belly growling in the elevator." She looped her purse strap over her neck and across her chest, then moved toward him and the door.

"You skipped dinner too?"

She glanced up at him in surprise. "Yeah. So did you?"

He nodded. "While you prepped equipment, I filled out forms. Excavating bodies on this scale means a lot of overtime. Among other things. But I'm done now and heading to Boone's to grab a burger." He looked down at her. "You?"

"That was my plan as well. One of their burgers with everything on it sounds amazing."

"Want to join me?"

Her eyes went wide, and she ducked her head, punching the button for the elevator before he could make out her expression. Did he really just ask her to go somewhere with him outside of work? After all the grief she gave him every day? He must be a glutton for punishment.

She pasted a smile on her face and looked up at him. "Haven't you had enough of me for the day?"

The elevator dinged, and they stepped inside. He glanced down at her, the crinkles popping out around his eyes as one corner of his mouth lifted. "I haven't seen much of you today, so I haven't gotten my quota in yet. I'm sure by the time we finish eating, I'll be ready for a break."

"Same, Doc. Same."

"So, does that mean you'll join me?"

She nodded. "Sure." Why not? She was a glutton for punishment too.

They rode the elevator up to the first floor and walked through the lobby and down a corridor to leave the hospital by the rear entrance.

"I'll meet you there," she told him as they reached the employee parking lot.

He nodded, peeling away toward the doctors' section, while she continued through the rows of cars to where she parked her little silver SUV this morning. It wasn't her first choice for a car—that would be a Mini Cooper—but a tiny British car was not at all practical in Colorado winters in the mountains. One day, she was going to buy one anyway, even if she could only drive it a few months out of the year.

She climbed inside her car, tossing her purse onto the passenger seat before starting the engine. Putting the SUV in gear, she headed for the exit just as Alex turned onto the main road in his much more expensive black SUV. They made a handful of turns before they pulled up in front of the small diner downtown. She parked out front next to him and got out.

He joined her on the sidewalk, his posture more relaxed now that they were away from work. She tried not to stare. Was she going to get a glimpse of the real Alex Randall? The not stick-in-the-mud she'd seen him be with the sheriff? Did she want to see that man? Resisting "boss Alex" was hard enough.

Readjusting her purse strap over her shoulder, she followed him into the restaurant.

Alex held the door for Katie as they entered the diner. The vanilla scent of her shampoo assaulted him as she walked past. He fought the urge to step up behind her and bury his nose in her hair. How did she still smell so good after working thirteen hours?

He planted his feet, letting some space open between them, then followed her. He should have just gotten his food to go. What was he thinking, eating with her? She drove him crazy—for many reasons, not the least of which was her desire to run *his* lab.

It was too late now to change his mind, though. She was already halfway across the diner. He followed her to a booth by the windows lining the side wall and sat down. They reached for menus as a young woman walked up, a notepad and pen in her hands.

Alex smiled at the girl, remembering her from the many other times he'd eaten at the diner.

"Hi, Becca."

She smiled back. "Hi, Dr. Randall. What can I get you to drink?"

"Iced tea, please."

She nodded, then looked at Katie.

"The same, please."

"Do you two know what you want to eat?"

Alex looked across the table at Katie in question.

"I just want a burger and fries. And a chocolate milkshake."

He smiled at her. "That sounds really good, actually." He

looked up at the girl. "I'll have the same, except make my shake strawberry."

The girl scribbled their order on her notepad. "Okay. I'll be back in a few with your drinks."

Katie put her menu away and sat back, then gazed out the window, drumming her fingers on the table.

"You know, we've worked together for over four years now, and I think this is the first time we've done anything together outside of work. Even in little get-togethers with other lab employees, we've never hung out," Alex said, leaning back.

She shrugged. "Technically, you're my boss."

He rolled his eyes. "Like that matters to you."

She giggled. "Well, if you did things my way, we wouldn't have any problems."

"Probably not," he chuckled. "But I also wouldn't have a job."

She narrowed her eyes, a teasing glint entering them. "Are you saying I'm not enough of a brown-noser?"

He laughed. "Yes. Very much."

"What can I say?" She leaned forward and crossed her arms on top of the table. "Politics were never my thing. Or people, for that matter. There's a reason I like working in a lab."

"I hear that. The dead don't talk back."

"Did you ever try to be a regular doctor?"

Alex nodded. "In med school. I went in with the full intention of becoming a surgeon. It didn't take me long to not only realize I didn't have the patience for, well, patients, but that I found forensics riveting. It was like a puzzle. Medicine is in general, really, but forensic pathology is one of those five-thousand-piece ones that are all black. There aren't many clues; just your own ability to identify patterns and things that aren't right."

"Yes!" She lifted a hand to point a finger at him. "Exactly. Being a criminalist is the same way. That's the best part of the job. Figuring out what's not right and why."

"Precisely."

"So, how did you end up here? You were in Salt Lake City. Why choose itty-bitty Silver Gap?"

"I'm from a small town in Oregon. I missed the atmosphere. Plus, I get to be my own boss for the most part. Though that does mean I have to deal with you."

She grinned. "Aren't you special?"

Becca walked up with their drinks and shakes, interrupting them. "Can I get you anything else right now?"

They both shook their heads, tearing open straws. Alex plunked one in his shake and took a deep draw.

"Cool. Your food should be up soon."

"Thanks, Becca," Katie said, putting a straw in her shake too. The girl smiled and walked away.

Alex swallowed another mouthful of his drink, curiosity getting the better of him as he watched the woman across from him. "So, are you from here? I inherited you when I took over, and I don't think I've ever asked if you're a native."

She shook her head. "I'm from Colorado Springs. I started working here right after I finished my master's, then took over as department head shortly before you arrived when our other one quit to move to Florida."

He shook his head. "You know, if I hadn't looked at your personnel file when I started, I wouldn't have known you had so little experience. You're very good at your job."

Her smile was shy, which surprised him. She had so much confidence when it came to her job, it seemed strange that she didn't when it came to herself.

"Thank you."

He picked up his shake and sat back. "That's also the only

reason I haven't fired you." He smiled around his straw, softening his words.

She pressed her lips together and glared at him. "Funny."

He grinned.

She rolled her eyes and took another drink. "What do you think we'll find tomorrow?"

"A mess." He set his glass down. "I'm just hoping for the low end Seb quoted me, which is four."

Katie's mouth pulled down, and she pushed her shake away. "I know you told me to prep for eight, but I'm really hoping there won't be any."

"Yeah, me too. Some people are sick." He sighed and picked up his shake again. "But that's why I do what I do. To bring the depraved to justice and give families closure."

She raised her glass. "Hear, hear."

Alex knocked his glass against hers and sucked down another mouthful of the thick shake. Becca walked up to their table carrying two plates of burgers and fries.

"Here you go." She set them down. "Can I get you anything else?"

They both shook their heads.

"I think we're good for now," Alex said.

The girl gave them a thumbs up. "Okay. Wave me down if you need anything." She whirled on her heel and walked away.

Both starving after the long day, they dove into their meals, conversation ceasing as they assuaged their hunger. But that didn't mean Alex didn't study her as they ate. She was an enigma. The woman was brilliant. But she didn't look like your typical brainiac. Shades of vibrant blue and purple threaded her naturally dark hair, and tattoos colored her arms. He was sure there were probably others he couldn't see. In her Converse sneakers and flannel shirts, she reminded him of a skater chick. A skater chick who would soon have a Ph.D.

"How's school going?" he asked. She'd told him about her

doctoral program, needing approval to be absent for certain days and times to attend classes, but he'd heard little about it since.

"It's good. I'm nearly done with my dissertation."

His eyebrows shot up. "Really? I didn't think you were that close to being finished."

"It's been two-and-a-half years since I started, so I would hope I'm about done."

"It's seriously been that long?"

She nodded.

He shook his head. "It doesn't feel like it. So, what's your topic?"

"The use of CRISPR as a tool for better DNA matching."

"Really?" That was an intriguing idea. "How so?"

"Using it on degraded samples that normal sequencing methods can't build a profile from because the chains are too busted up and piecing them together creates errors. CRISPR allows for the accuracy in reassembly that other techniques lack."

"Have you had any success?"

She nodded. "Seb let me use the county's DNA database. I compiled cases where DNA evidence was used to convict a subject, got permission from the convict and the victim if one was directly involved, and ran the DNA using my technique. It's confirmed the cases that were a complete match, several that were only partial, and I exonerated two others."

"And it held up in court?"

"No, because it isn't an approved technique yet. But it gave the lawyers a reason to appeal. Through that, the police reopened the cases and found additional evidence."

Alex sat back and stared at her. "How did I not know about this?"

She shrugged. "I did most of the work after you left for the day. I would stay late. Or, I went to the university and worked on it there. It was separate from my duties in the lab, so it's not really something you would need to know about."

"So, all those late nights you pulled early this year and last year, you were working on that?"

She nodded.

He glanced out over the restaurant in a bit of awe. Both at her idea and her work ethic. He looked back at her. "I think once you get your Ph.D., I'm going to have to ask the county council to take forensics out from under my purview, your aversion to brown-nosing be dammed. You're probably already better qualified to make the decisions for your department than I am."

She grinned and stuffed a fry in her mouth. "I've been telling you that since day one."

"Yeah, but now it's true."

Katie narrowed her eyes at him, but her smile spoiled the look. Alex glanced down at his plate, surprised to see all his food gone except a couple of fries. He thought he'd be in for a long, boring dinner he couldn't wait to get away from. But the opposite was true. He didn't want to go home.

Becca strolled back up to their table, pulling him out of his thoughts.

"You guys want any dessert?"

Katie patted her stomach. "I'm stuffed, so none for me."

Alex cleared his throat. "I'll pass too."

The girl nodded and tore their check off her notepad, laying it face down on the table. "I can check you out at the counter when you're ready."

They thanked her, and she walked away. Alex reached for the check, his hand closing over Katie's as she did too. Startled at the contact, he looked up at her. She stared back at him, wide-eyed.

He cleared his throat. "I'll get the bill. You are a struggling grad student, after all." He cracked a joke to dispel the sudden tension.

She laughed and withdrew her hand, motioning to the check. "Go for it." He picked it up and slid toward the edge of the booth. "Are you ready to go?"

"Yeah." She drained the last of her shake and picked up her purse, then slid out of the booth.

He paid for their meal, and they walked outside. Stopping in front of their cars, he fidgeted with the keys in his pocket, things suddenly awkward.

"I guess I'll see you in the morning." She jangled her keys.

Alex nodded. "Yeah. Um, have a good night."

"I will. You too."

They stood there for a moment longer before he backed away with a nod. As he climbed into his car, he glanced at her through the passenger window. Light from the interior of her car lit up her face as she got inside, glinting off her glasses and hair. Colorful tresses fanned over her shoulder as she closed the door. She was so far from his type, but he'd be damned if there wasn't a knot of attraction in his belly now after their dinner together. Shaking his head, not quite sure what to make of this sudden infatuation, he looked away and started his car.

Two

Katie spared Alex a glance as he walked into the lab dressed for a hike. Her eyes about bugged out of her head as she took in his denim-clad legs and flannel-covered chest. A white, long-sleeved shirt peeked out from the neckline and the rolled-up sleeves of his button down. His forearms flexed as he flipped through his keys to find the one for his office door. He looked like a lumberjack. A sexy one.

When her feet took a step in his direction without her permission, she looked away and focused on putting the last few items into the plastic tote, so she could have one of her staff take it down to the loading dock and put it in the forensics' van. Ogling Alex would have to wait; she had a job to do.

Getting the last of the supplies they might need for their expedition loaded up, she followed her techs to the dock. They put the last few totes inside and closed the doors. She rounded the vehicle to get in the driver's seat, but stopped short when she saw Alex standing there. He held up the van keys.

"I'll drive."

"What? No." She held out her hand. "Give me the keys. It's my van."

"I'm your boss, remember?"

Katie rolled her eyes. "We're back to this now? Last night, you said I should be the boss."

"Yes, but you're not. Not yet."

She huffed and put her hands on her hips. "Alex, just give me the damn keys. We're wasting time."

"Agreed." He pulled open the door and hopped inside.

She stared at him.

He arched a brow at her. "Get in."

Katie huffed again and stomped around the front of the vehicle to climb into the passenger seat. She snapped her seatbelt into place as he started the engine.

"The rest of the team is following us, yes?"

"Yeah. Devin's driving them in one of the county's transport vans."

"Awesome. Let's hit the road, then." He put the van in gear while she fumed silently beside him. She thought they were past this boss-employee B.S.

Turning out of the lot, they started the hour and a half journey into the mountains to the Paulsons' property. She stared out the window, watching the scenery while trying to ignore Alex in all his lumberjack glory next to her. Her anger that he pulled rank on her helped.

She didn't know why it upset her so much. Maybe because she thought they moved into new territory last night, and now he was back to being her stick-in-the-mud boss again.

"That coffee in the cup holder there is for you." His low voice broke the silence.

She glanced at the console between them to see two cups of coffee from Peppy Brewster sitting there. "Thanks," she muttered and looked back out the window.

Alex sighed. "It's going to be a long ride if you won't talk to me."

She shrugged. "I like the scenery."

"Uh-huh. Sure. I'm getting the cold shoulder because you like the scenery. You can't be that upset I wouldn't let you drive."

She looked at him then. "It's not about that. It's about you pulling rank. I thought you saw me as an equal. My bad, *Dr. Randall*."

He groaned and rested his head against the seat. "I do see you as an equal. I just don't like letting anyone drive me anywhere, so I pulled rank."

She frowned. "Why didn't you just say that, then?"

"Because it's easier to not explain."

Katie grinned, her ire forgotten as she sensed a story. "Make it up to me and enlighten me."

He huffed, looking at her. "You're not going to let me get away with just that explanation, are you?"

"Nope."

"Fine." He huffed again. "I was in a nasty car accident in my teens. A buddy and I were on our way to a party after a football game. He offered to drive, even though I planned on driving myself. But it would save me some gas money, so I let him. He got distracted, messing with the radio, and misjudged a curve in the road. We went over an embankment and down a hill before coming to a stop on the beach. The car landed in the surf. If there hadn't been people partying on that beach, I would have drowned. As it was, my friend didn't survive."

Katie gasped and covered her mouth. "Oh my goodness. How badly were you hurt?"

"Broken pelvis and femur. And I had a severe concussion and two cracked vertebrae. My friend broke his neck in the crash. They said he died instantly." Alex sighed. "But that's why I don't like to let anyone else drive. I figure if I'm going to crash, it's going to be my own fault, or something I can't see coming." He looked at her again. "Am I forgiven?"

She fluttered a hand. "I suppose." Her expression sobered. "I'm sorry about your friend."

Alex shrugged and gave a short nod. "It was a long time ago, but thank you. So, are you going to talk to me now?"

Katie giggled. "About what?"

"Tell me about yourself. We've worked together four years and all I know is you're good at your job, brilliant, and from Colorado Springs."

She relaxed into her seat. "There isn't much to tell, really. I grew up pathetically normal. My parents were both science teachers. I have a younger brother named Zeke. He's a park ranger by day and competes professionally as a rock climber."

"Wait. Your younger brother is Zeke Mitchum?"

She nodded. "You've heard of him?"

"Yeah. I do quite a bit of rock climbing. He's a big name in the sport. Do you climb?"

"Some. I'm not a fanatic for it like he is, but I've done my fair share."

"We should go sometime. I haven't been out in a while and it would be nice to get a climb in before the weather turns. Tell me something else. You mentioned an ex once."

She blinked twice as her brain registered the fact he wanted to go somewhere with her, then the abrupt change in subject. "Um, yeah. I was married for a hot minute in grad school. The first time I was in grad school," she amended. "Jonas was a fellow criminology student. We'd been dating several months and moved in together when my roommate moved in with her boyfriend. After a few months of cohabitating, we got married. It was spur of the moment, but I quickly realized he just wanted to ride my coattails. He was the one to suggest moving in together—I had the nicer apartment. I was also doing much better in school. He was in danger of flunking out because he liked to party too much. That should have been a red flag for me, but he was sweet. Right up until I divorced him."

Alex frowned at her. "Did he hurt you?"

"Not physically. But he hurled some nice insults my way. Told me no man would ever want me because I looked like a tatted up biker's bitch. And that now I didn't even have him because there was no way he'd take me back."

He scoffed. "His loss. You're sexy as hell."

Katie's eyes went wide. A flush crept up Alex's neck, and he looked at her askance.

"I'm sorry. That was not appropriate," he said.

She rolled her lips in, her own face reddening. "You think I'm sexy?" she asked, her voice quiet.

He arched a brow and glanced at her. "Have you looked in a mirror?"

She blushed harder. "Please. I'm nothing special. A man like you, I'm sure you've had your pick of beautiful, sophisticated women."

"I have. And I think you could hold your own."

A small thrill went through her at the heat in his eyes. She glanced back out the window and cleared her throat. "Thank you."

Silence enveloped them for a moment before he broke it again.

"Why do you have all the tattoos, if you don't mind me asking? I don't have anything against them; I'm just curious. It's not something you see often on a woman. Especially not one so... bookish."

Katie looked down at her arms and the colorful artwork covering them. "I like art. I draw a lot in my free time." She shrugged. "It felt right to put some of that on my body. I don't regret any of them."

"You shouldn't. They're beautiful. Even more so now that I know you drew them."

Uncomfortable being the center of attention, she turned the conversation to him. "Your turn. Tell me about yourself."

He sighed. "My upbringing is a lot like yours, except my mom was an accountant and my dad owned a garage. I have a younger sister. She's a math teacher and married to her high school sweetheart."

"Did you always want to be a doctor?"

"No. I wanted to be a mechanic like my dad until I was in that car accident. Getting an up-close view of the profession piqued my interest. I started taking more advanced science classes the next school year and loved every minute of it."

"Hmm. What about relationships? Have you ever been married?"

He shook his head. "No. I came close once. I was engaged for about a year. She was a doctor too. But our schedules never synced, and we just drifted apart."

That woman was stupid. Alex Randall was a great catch. If he were hers, she'd never let him go. If scheduling was a problem, she'd find a way to make it not a problem.

But he wasn't and wouldn't ever be. They were barely friends.

Alex pulled into the Paulsons' drive and wove his way through the trees into the clearing around the house and outbuildings. Katie stared out the windshield at the myriad of law enforcement vehicles already on-site, including the sheriff, Sebastian Archer, and his chief deputy, Jace Travers. The two men stood in front of the sheriff's SUV, looking at a map spread over the hood. Alex steered the van toward them and parked.

"Let's do this," Katie said, climbing out of the vehicle.

Seb and Jace waved at them as they came around the front of the van.

"You have a plan?" Alex asked, with a nod at the map.

"Basic grid search," Seb replied. "We're going to start with the cadaver dog on one side and Katie with the radar unit on the other and meet in the middle. You and Dr. Pressley can just hang out while we comb the property until we find something."

"Amanda's here already?" Alex looked around.

Jace pointed to a set of two dark blue SUVs sporting the University of Colorado logo. "She's over there with her team."

Alex nudged her arm. "Come on. I'll introduce you."

She nodded.

"Five minutes and we're going to get started," Seb said. "The state boys just got here, too, with their dog, so we're all set now."

"We'll let her know," Alex said.

Katie followed him across the grass to the SUV. As they neared, a blonde woman in tight black jeans, hiking boots, and a windbreaker emblazoned with the university's logo stepped around the side of the car. Katie's step faltered. This was the bone doctor? She glanced at Alex.

"Mandy!" He grinned and raised a hand in greeting.

The woman looked over, a bright smile blossoming on her pretty face. "Hey, you. Glad you could finally join us."

Alex rolled his eyes. "Like you beat me here by much." He leaned in and gave her a hug.

Katie stood back, staring at the pair. When they continued to converse, ignoring her, she cleared her throat.

"Oh!" Alex glanced back. "Sorry. Mandy, this is Katie Mitchum, chief of forensics. Katie, this is Amanda Pressley."

Katie held out a hand. "It's nice to meet you, doctor."

"Call me Amanda, please." Her cornflower blue eyes sparkled. "It's nice to meet you, too."

Jesus, it's Dr. Barbie. Katie fought not to roll her eyes.

"Are you guys ready?" Alex asked. "Seb's ready to roll."

Amanda nodded. "Yep." She turned and let out a whistle. Two men and a woman looked up and started walking toward them. "This is my team. Chelsea, Owen, and Dave."

Katie and Alex introduced themselves.

"Let's go see where Seb wants us, shall we?" Alex said.

Eager to get away from the perky blonde and the goofy smile still on Alex's face, she spun on her heel and marched back to the sheriff and his deputy.

After getting directions on where to start, Katie pushed Amanda and Alex from her mind and snagged her favorite tech, Devin, to help her with the radar. Everyone else was on hold until they located something.

Approaching the edge of the woods, she turned on the radar, taking some readings to calibrate the machine.

"Everything good, Katie?" Jace asked.

"Yep. Just checking the settings. Let's go." She pushed the machine forward, moving at a slow but steady pace.

Before long, Katie zoned into her work, pushing all other thoughts from her mind as she walked and watched the monitor. She wanted to do the children buried here justice; they deserved her full attention. After two hours of walking, the image she'd been dreading to see appeared on the screen.

"Jace." She stopped and glanced over at the deputy, pointing at the monitor.

His mouth flattened and turned down as he took in the small skeleton on the screen. "Dammit." He lifted his radio and called for Seb and the two doctors to make their way to them.

Katie pushed a flag into the ground next to the radar and studied the surrounding area. Several spots of new growth caught her attention. She headed for the closest one.

"Katie?"

She pointed at the area sprouting several small saplings. "See the new growth?"

He nodded, looking around, noticing what they hadn't before. "There's more than one spot."

"Yep." She maneuvered the machine into the saplings and another body appeared on her screen. She sighed and looked at Jace. "Pull the K-9 from its current location. I think we found the burial ground."

Expression grim, Jace nodded and lifted his radio again.

Gravel crunched beneath Alex's boots as he walked toward the forensics van. He was dead on his feet. And starving. The bagged lunches they brought were a long time ago.

He walked up to the driver's door, reaching for the handle, but paused at the sight of Katie sitting behind the wheel. With a frown, he rapped his knuckles on the window. It rolled down, and she gave him a sweet smile.

"Yes?"

"We talked about this on the way here. Get out so I can drive."

She looked at him over the top of her glasses. "Step out of your comfort zone, Alex. Get in."

"Katie..."

She grinned and rolled the window up.

Alex growled and whirled away, walking around the front of the van to get in the passenger seat. He slammed the door shut, scowling.

"Oh, cheer up," she said, cranking the engine. "You can take a nap on the way back."

"I don't want to nap. I want to drive." He fastened his seatbelt and tried to settle into the seat.

"Are you going to be this grouchy the whole way home?"

He shrugged. "I hope you're ready for a side-seat driver."

She arched a brow at him. "You're seriously going to

comment on my driving the entire way? We both know how well I take directions."

He flashed a smile. "Then let me drive."

"Nice try," she said with a laugh. Shifting into gear, she headed down the drive behind Seb's vehicle.

Alex gripped the center armrest with one hand, his knuckles going white. Maybe he should just close his eyes like she suggested. He tipped his head back against the headrest and did just that. The van bumped over a dip in the drive.

Nope, that was worse. His eyes snapped open, and he sat up.

"Sorry," Katie muttered. "This driveway isn't in the best condition."

"Hadn't noticed," he said through gritted teeth.

She glanced at him, then sighed. "Fine." She pulled to a stop.

"What?"

"You can drive." She unfastened her seatbelt and opened her door.

A bit confused, but not willing to argue, he climbed out, changing positions with her.

"Feel better?" she asked as he put the car in gear.

"Much. Thank you."

Katie crossed her arms and closed her eyes.

"Why'd you change your mind?"

"Because I thought you might have a heart attack before we got back if I didn't. You about shot through the roof when I hit that pothole."

He sighed. "I know it's something I need to work on, but it isn't usually an issue." He glanced at her with a glare.

One corner of her mouth lifted, but her eyes stayed closed.

Alex blew out a breath, shaking his head. She sure knew how to push his buttons.

"So are you going to go to sleep on me now, since you aren't driving?"

"Maybe. Do you want me to stay awake?"

"No. Sleep if you want. You put in a long day." They'd found six bodies in the same area and were bringing two back with them today. They still needed to comb the rest of the property, but he was hoping there was only the one burial site.

"So did you. You *and* Dr. Pressley." She opened her eyes. "Speaking of, we need to make some more room when we get back so she can spread out tomorrow."

"Oh, so you'll make room for Mandy, but not me? I see how it is." A smile teased his mouth.

Katie smiled back. "I don't know her as well, so I don't want to rock the boat. And why do you call her Mandy when she introduced herself as Amanda?"

"I've known her several years. Both being in forensics, we cross paths at conferences now and then. And we might have gone on a few dates over the years," he admitted.

"Dates?"

"Yes, dates."

"That's all?"

"Yes." He glanced at her with a frown. "Why are you so curious? Jealous?"

She scoffed and crossed her arms. "No."

Even in the dim light from the dashboard lights, Alex could tell she was blushing. He didn't mind that she was jealous. She might drive him nuts with her desire to run the lab her way, but he found her brilliant and intriguing. Not to mention sexy. More so now that he was making an effort to get to know her.

"So, why isn't it more?" Her voice was quiet, barely audible over the hum of the tires on the road.

Alex shrugged. "Probably for the same reason my engagement failed. Time constraints. And we live in different cities."

"Denver isn't that far. You could live in between."

"That's still an hour either way in good weather. I like Mandy, but we're better as friends."

"Why?"

"She's not really interested in anything long-term. I am."

"But if she were?"

He shrugged again. "Maybe. But she isn't going to change her tune, and I can't see either of us wanting to move for the other, so it's moot."

Katie hummed and closed her eyes again. "Well, I think you make a cute couple. You should work on that."

Alex rolled his eyes. "I'll get right on that, thanks."

Her mouth quirked. "Good boy."

He couldn't help himself and laughed.

"Shhh. I'm trying to sleep." She waved a hand at him, fighting a grin.

"Mmm-hmm." He shook his head, smiling, but stayed quiet. The peace in the van was nice compared to the hectic pace of their day. Not to mention the heartbreak. A couple of those skeletons were rather small. He couldn't imagine how depraved someone needed to be to rape and murder a child. He, Amanda, and Katie would do everything they could to give those children justice.

THREE

Alex nudged Katie awake as he turned off the van. "Hey. We're back."

She drew in a deep breath and stretched. "Oh. I really did fall asleep."

"You did. Now I'm doubly glad you let me drive."

She rolled her eyes and took off her seatbelt, pulling on the door handle to get out. "I would have stayed awake fine if I'd driven."

"Maybe." He pushed his own door open and climbed out.

Another set of headlights lit up the parking lot as Devin pulled in. He parked beside the van and the forensic techs poured out, yawning and moaning about being stiff.

Katie clapped her hands. "Let's get unloaded so we can all go home and get some sleep."

Two more vehicles pulled in, carrying Dr. Pressley and her team. Her car was barely in park before she jumped out and hurried over to the forensics van.

"Be careful! We don't want to cause any damage to the bones."

Alex frowned as he eyed the forensics team. They were doing fine. They hadn't even touched the remains yet.

Katie stepped forward. "My team knows what they're doing, Amanda."

The other woman frowned but nodded. "I'm sure they do. I was just cautioning them. Damage could make it difficult to determine cause of death."

"We're aware," Alex said, stepping forward. He didn't like her tone. "Do you have a problem with the way my people work?"

Amanda smiled, her expression forced. "Of course not, Alex. It's been a long day. How about my team gives you a hand?" She stepped around him, motioning to her techs before he could say anything.

He turned to watch her, wondering why she was acting so peculiar.

"What's her problem? She was all perky at the site."

"I'm not sure. I don't know what's going on with her. She's not normally so—"

"Shrill?"

"Yeah."

She glanced up at him, and he looked down to meet her gaze. "Well, you might want to caution her to be nice to my team. It might be your lab, but those are my people. I won't stand for her being rude or dictatorial to them. I'll throw her ass out, case be damned. She's not the only forensic anthropologist in the western states."

"Noted. I'll talk to her. Maybe she really is just tired."

"Hmm. Maybe." She cast one last look at him before sauntering away to help her team.

Alex sighed and scrubbed his hands over his face. How did he end up with two difficult women in his lab?

∾

Katie kept one eye on Amanda as they unloaded the van. The doctor stood off to the side, watching them all as they worked, offering an occasional "suggestion." After the third time she told one of her techs how to do their job, Katie decided she'd had enough.

"How about you help instead of micromanaging?" She thrust a plastic tote full of dirt samples at the woman.

"Oh!" Amanda scrabbled to get a better grip on it as Katie let go and stepped away. "Well, that was rude."

"No ruder than you've been to my team. Stop telling them how to do their jobs. I picked the best and trained them to be better. They know what they're doing."

Amanda huffed, her face tight, but she walked through the door at the loading dock without a word.

Yeah, this case was going to be a blast, Katie mused, following her inside with another tote. She stacked her box next to Amanda's on a cart and went back out for another one. Once they off-loaded all the evidence, they could finally get to the two bodies they removed from their shallow graves.

Katie hopped up into the van, Alex behind her, and reached for the first body bag on the shelves lining the walls. She unhooked the straps holding it in place and slid it toward the edge of the shelf. The van bounced as Amanda stepped inside.

"Careful!"

She let go of the bag and glared at the other woman. "Okay. What is your problem?"

"Nothing. I just don't want to see any damage."

"Why are you so sure I'm going to damage the remains?"

Amanda bit her lip and waved a hand at her. "You're, well —" She broke off and shrugged.

Katie narrowed her eyes, beginning to get a clearer picture of what was going on. "I'm what? And think very carefully about what you say. I'm tired, hungry, and one hundred percent done with this day."

"Mandy, do you have a problem with Katie?"

The other woman crossed her arms and shrugged again. "I mean, look at her, Alex. How good can someone like her be?"

Her ex's words ricocheted through Katie's mind and to her horror, she felt tears prick her eyes. Doing her best to keep it together, Katie gave the other woman a tight smile. "Well, I think I'm done here." She looked at Alex. "I think Dr. Elitist can handle things now." She pushed past him and hopped out of the van.

"Katie."

She didn't turn around at Alex calling her. Instead, she let out a sharp whistle, signaling her team. Several heads turned in her direction.

"My team, go home. Dr. Pressley's crew will take over." She marched past several stunned faces and into the building.

"Katie, wait!"

Alex's boots thudded over the asphalt, but she didn't slow down or turn around. Whether it was fatigue or the emotional rollercoaster of finding six dead children or a combination of both, Amanda Pressley's remarks had stripped away the final thread holding her emotions together. She was done.

A firm hand took hold of her arm.

"Let me go, Alex." She kept her eyes on the top button of his shirt, knowing if she looked at him, she wouldn't be able to hold in her emotions. He drove her crazy, but she trusted him. That connection would be all that was necessary to pull the cork on her tears.

"No. Don't run away. I'll handle Amanda and make it clear she's very wrong. I need—want you to stay."

She glanced up at him then, hearing the softer quality in his voice. His deep blue eyes watched her, a tender and imploring expression on his face.

"Please stay?"

Katie sighed. "Fine. But she has to stay out of my way. If she can't handle that—handle me—she can take herself off this case. I meant what I said. There *are* other forensic anthropologists we can call to help."

"I know, and I'll make that abundantly clear. I'm not sure what's going on."

She grunted and walked around him. "Come on. I just want to get all this evidence stored inside and go home."

As she stepped outside, her assistant, Devin, walked up. "Katie? Do you really want us all to leave? There's still a lot of work left."

She shook her head. "No. It was just a misunderstanding. Let's finish up."

He nodded and motioned to the rest of the team. They followed her back to the evidence van. She climbed back inside with Amanda, who stood with one of the bodies, bent over it and peering inside the body bag.

"What are you doing?" Katie asked.

The other woman straightened and turned. "Nothing. Just waiting for some help."

Katie narrowed her eyes. "And you just decided to look inside the body bag while you waited?"

Amanda fidgeted with the zipper, pulling it closed, her eyes looking everywhere but at Katie. "Just getting a head start on my exam. Can we get back to work, please?"

Katie stared at her for a moment. Something about her explanation felt fishy. She made a mental note to talk to Seb about the pretty doctor, but let it go for now. "Sure. You going to stop treating me like a felon?"

Amanda's spine straightened and her eyes turned flinty. "Fine."

"Good. Glad we have an understanding. Grab that end."

She pointed to the body bag, then reached for the end closest to her. With Amanda's help, they slid the body off the shelf and backed out of the van to place it on a gurney one of Katie's team members brought out. Alex and Devin climbed in after them to get the next one, placing it on a second gurney. They wheeled them all inside, where Alex stowed them in the morgue fridge. Her techs followed with the carts full of evidence from the scene. When everything was in the lab, there was little room to move.

"We're going to have to do something about this," Alex muttered to her.

"Yeah. Tomorrow. We'll do something about it tomorrow. Or the next day, since we have to be back out at the property first thing in the morning." She rubbed her face and smoothed her hair back with a sigh. "I think that's everything. Let's go home."

"I like that idea." Alex rolled his head. "Thanks for all your hard work, everyone," he said, raising his voice. "Go home and get some rest."

Katie's team waved and filtered out, leaving them with Amanda and her crew.

"Are you driving back to Denver?" Alex asked them.

Amanda shook her head. "No. We're staying at that bed-and-breakfast just outside of town. The Lilac Inn."

"The sheriff's wife runs that place. You'll like it," Katie said.

"So long as it has a bed and a hot shower, I don't care," Chelsea quipped. "Are we ready to go, Dr. Pressley?"

Amanda's eyes drifted to the fridge for a split second, but she nodded. "Yeah. Let's get some rest."

"We'll walk you out," Alex said, taking a step toward the door.

Katie's hand shot out to touch his arm. He glanced at her. "Actually, could I talk to you for a minute?"

His brow creased, but he nodded before looking at Amanda. "We'll see you guys tomorrow."

She smiled at them, but Katie wasn't fooled. It was forced. There was something hinky going on.

"Goodnight," Amanda murmured and followed her team out the door.

Katie whirled to look up at Alex as soon as the door swished shut. "We need to keep a close eye on her when she's with the bodies and evidence."

He frowned down at her. "What? Why?"

"After I agreed to stay and went back to the van, I caught her looking inside one of the body bags."

His frown deepened. "Why would she be looking in one of the bags while they were still in the van?"

"That's a good question. I asked her what she was doing, and she said she was just getting a head start on her examination."

"What? That doesn't make any sense."

"No, it doesn't, which is why we need to be with her when she's with the evidence. I know she's your friend, but I don't trust her. She's up to something. I'm going to ask Seb to look into her background. See if she has a connection to this case in some way."

He blew out a breath and ran a hand through his hair. "I highly doubt she's mixed up in anything illegal. This case is just probably getting to her like it is the rest of us."

Katie pursed her lips, staring at the door. "Maybe. But we're not sneaking peeks in a body bag and treating our co-workers like felons."

Alex sighed again. "I'm sure there's a logical explanation. Can we just go get some dinner now and go home?"

She gave him a sharp look. "You want to go to dinner with me again?"

"You know we're both headed to Boone's, so why not?"

"Maybe I want to get mine to go."

"Do you?"

Not if it meant missing out on sitting across from him again. But she also really just wanted to sink into her bathtub with a slice of pizza and a glass of wine.

"How about a compromise? Today calls for wine and comfort food. I really want pizza. How about we share one?"

"Where? There aren't any sit-down pizza places in town. It's all carry-out."

"Um, here?"

He shook his head. "We can't have alcohol. And I need a stiff drink."

"Same. Okay. One of our houses, then? I think mine's the closest."

Alex tilted his head and stared down at her. "You sure? I mean, I know we tore down some barriers yesterday with our dinner at Boone's, but we aren't exactly friends."

Katie shrugged and toyed with the ends of her hair hanging over her shoulder. "Maybe not, but I don't want to be alone yet, and you get it." It was the only explanation she could come up with for her sudden desire to override her common sense. Getting close to Alex Randall would not be healthy for her emotional wellbeing, but she couldn't bring herself to care. He understood what she felt right now. She needed that to help purge the images of those tiny, skeletonized bodies in their shallow graves.

He straightened, understanding crossing his handsome face, and nodded. "Okay. I'll pick up the pizza if you get the wine? Or beer? I'm not really picky."

"Beer goes better with pizza." It also didn't go to her head as fast. She'd save the wine for later when she sank into a tub full of bubbles after he left.

"Sounds good. What do you want on your pizza?"

"Whatever you want is fine. I'll eat just about anything."

She pointed a finger at him. "Except pineapple or anchovies."

He grinned. "How's pepperoni and sausage sound?"

"Perfect."

Alex took his phone from his pocket. "I'll call it in."

"I'll go get the beer and see you at my house. Do you know where I live?"

"The general area, but not the address."

She rattled it off as she retreated to the doors. "Make sure you tell the night shift guys to keep an eye on things. Just in case Dr. Pressley decides she wants to get another head start on her autopsies."

He frowned, but nodded. "I still think you're seeing things that aren't there, but I'll tell them to stay vigilant."

"Thanks." She waved and walked out. As the door closed behind her, she couldn't help but wonder what she'd just done. Being with Alex in a public diner after work had tested her willpower. What would having him in her house do?

Alex tipped his bottle up, draining the last of his beer as he walked around Katie's living room looking at all her art on display. Pencil sketches lined the walls, some of them in color, but most in black and white. They ran the gamut on themes. She'd drawn everything from an owl feather to portraits of her family to the mountain range that surrounded Silver Gap.

"Why did you go into forensics? Why not art?" He gestured to the framed drawings.

She wandered over to stand next to him and looked at the sketches. "There's little money in it. I would have to crank out a lot of these every month—and sell them—to make what I do now. I doubt my work would go that quickly. Plus, I like forensics. I like helping people."

"Well, if you have to have a hobby, I suppose it's a good

one." He glanced down at her. "You're very talented."

She blushed and looked away. "Thanks."

There was that insecurity again, he noted. He wondered what caused it. She had no reason to be uncertain of herself; she was both brilliant and talented.

"You should hang some of these in the lab." An idea hit him. "Say, could you do a medical themed set for my office?"

She glanced up at him, her eyes wide with surprise. "You want to hang my drawings in your office?"

"Well, yeah. They're amazing."

Her eyes traveled between him and the wall of art, then back. "They're okay, but I wouldn't call them amazing."

"Seriously?" He frowned down at her. "Katie, I don't know where this misguided perception you have of your art comes from, but you're dead wrong."

She looked at the sketches again, her head tilting as she studied them through his eyes for a moment before she shrugged. "If you say so. I'm happy to draw something for you if you want, though."

"I do."

Katie walked over to the couch and sat down, picking up a sketchbook from the coffee table. She patted the cushion next to her. "Come tell me what you want."

"You want to do them now?" He walked over and sat down, leaning his elbows on his knees. He rolled his empty bottle in his hands as he watched her flip to a blank page.

"I can start them. It'll take me more than an evening to get them right, though." She glanced up at him, her glasses sliding down her nose.

Damn, she looked cute sitting there like that. All sexy librarian-ish. He took a deep breath through his nose to clear his head and focused his gaze on the paper. "Can you do an anatomy sketch? Like of the heart or brain or something?"

She nodded. "Let's do the heart." With swift strokes, she

outlined a heart on the page, then flipped to the next one and glanced up at him, a question in her pretty hazel eyes.

"Medical instruments?"

Wordlessly, she roughed out a grouping of a scalpel, stethoscope, and some clamps.

"I probably have enough wall space for four drawings. What about a skeleton on one and the Caduceus for the fourth?" he said, mentioning the universal symbol of medicine.

She nodded. "That would look good," she said, continuing to draw as she talked. "If you group them two by two, it will balance the instruments well."

He leaned back, watching her sketch. She was like a different woman when she was absorbed in her art. There was a softness about her that was missing when she was engrossed in a task in the lab. But the crease in her brow as she concentrated was the same. Her tongue peeked out to touch the corner of her mouth as she drew, and Alex's heart rate picked up.

Katie paused to examine her drawing, then glanced at him. He wasn't quick enough to avert his eyes, and she caught him staring at her mouth. Her eyes widened a fraction, and her breath hitched ever so slightly. It was enough to tell him she felt this insane, sudden attraction too.

He shifted, setting his bottle on the table, then leaned toward her. His fingers skimmed her knee as he turned. She watched him as he bent closer, her gaze flickering between his eyes and his mouth as it descended toward hers. With just a few inches between them, he paused, wanting to be sure she wanted this as much as he did. When her eyes met his again, they blazed with heat. He closed the distance and pressed his lips to hers.

~

Holy shit! Disbelief ping-ponged through Katie's head as Alex kissed her. Desire was fast on its heels as the feel of his warm, supple mouth on hers registered. Her thoughts scattered, and she dropped her pencil to clutch fistfuls of his shirt, holding herself steady as he nipped at her bottom lip, then soothed the bite with his tongue. He elicited a gasp from her as he threaded one hand through the strands of her ponytail, wrapping his fist in it and angling her head for better access. He took full advantage and tasted the inner recesses of her mouth. She returned the favor, noting the lingering taste of bright hops and tangy pizza sauce.

He pulled back to stare down at her, his normally bright blue eyes the color of the twilight sky. His chest heaved as he sucked in air, matching hers breath for breath.

"Damn."

Understatement of the century.

She licked her lips, tasting him as she stared back. His eyes followed the movement, getting impossibly darker before his mouth crashed back onto hers. He didn't hold back this time, wrapping his arms around her and pulling her half onto his lap. Katie twined her arms around his neck and grasped his dark hair, raking her nails over his scalp as he invaded her mouth, plundering its depths. Who knew Mr. Stick-in-the-mud had this in him?

Her sketchbook fell to the floor with a soft thud as she turned and tucked one leg up on the couch. Alex's hands drifted down her back to hold her butt, urging her in closer. As she straddled his lap and felt the evidence of his desire, rationality crashed back into her, and she broke their kiss. Breathing hard, she rested her forehead against his.

"What are we doing?"

"Isn't it obvious?" he asked. "We're moving straight past the friends stage."

She lifted her head to look down at him, searching his eyes.

"As nice as that was, I'm not sure it's a great idea. We work together."

He sighed. "I know. I had the same thought before you threaded your fingers through my hair. Then I couldn't think at all. So, what do we do about this?" His hands were still on her hips, and he pressed her down a fraction so she could feel what she did to him.

Katie bit back a moan. He played dirty! But sex—at least at this stage—would do more harm than good. A few days ago, they were at each other's throats constantly. What would happen when the passion inevitably settled into a deep burn instead of the flash in the pan it was now? If they didn't build a relationship first and work on their issues, they were doomed.

Mustering up every ounce of willpower she had, she broke free of his hold and stood, backing away. "I think we leave it at this for now."

He didn't move off the couch. Just stared up at her with an arched brow. "Yeah?"

She tried not to let her eyes wander, but it was hard to ignore the bulge in his pants. She swallowed hard. "Yeah."

He held her gaze another moment, then stood, taking two steps toward her. "I'll see you tomorrow." His voice was low and soft, like his eyes. He reached out with one finger and brushed a tendril of her hair from her face, then leaned in and placed a gentle kiss on her lips. "Goodnight."

"Goodnight," she whispered back.

He walked around her, heading for the door. She turned to watch him go, not moving until the door closed behind him. When it clicked shut, her breath left her on a whoosh. She spun, backpedaling a few steps, and collapsed onto the couch, her muscles turning to mush as the adrenaline left.

Her head fell back against the cushions and she stared up at the ceiling. What the fuck just happened?

Four

Katie glanced at the clock for the tenth time in as many minutes. They were back at the lab, processing evidence, and it was getting late. She was ready to leave, but Amanda was determined to finish processing a second body. Alex was assisting, and Katie didn't want to leave without talking to him about what they found so far. She told Seb her concerns about Amanda earlier, and he said he'd look into her background.

She was still acting strange, hurrying through some steps and bodies, while taking a painstaking amount of time with others. Katie had a feeling she was looking for something specific. She just wished she knew what. After yesterday, though, she wasn't about to talk to the woman unless she had to. It wasn't the first time she'd faced some prejudice for the way she looked, but it was the first time it really bothered her, and it all had to do with Alex. She didn't want him to start doubting her abilities because someone whom he considered a friend did.

With a sigh, she looked at the clock again. A minute had

ticked by. Grumbling under her breath, she picked up a bone sample she just prepped from the body Alex and Amanda were working on, and put it in her brand-new gas chromatograph to see what it could tell her. While she waited on the machine to do its magic, she tidied up her workstation. Hopefully, by the time the test was done, they would be too.

While she worked, she tried not to peek at the clock again. Instead, she focused on her job, finding small tasks to keep her busy. Part way through her tidying up process, she flipped the sample over to the mass spectrometer, hoping to get some accurate dating on it. By the time it finished running, she was watching the clock again. There were only so many things she could clean.

She hit the button on the machine to compile a report, then sat down at her desk to open the file. Reading the results, she cocked her head. *Strange...*

"Hey, guys. You need to see this."

"What is it?" Amanda asked, her voice sharp. "We're busy."

Katie gritted her teeth. She glanced back to toss the woman a glare.

Alex frowned at Amanda, then stripped off his gloves and walked over to Katie's desk. "What did you find?"

She pointed at the screen. "That body you're working on is considerably older than the other two. She's also been moved from her original grave."

"Shit, so there could be more?"

"Potentially, yes. The mineral composition of the dirt samples from around her body don't match what I would expect to have leeched into her bones. Can you find a dirt sample from a joint? Some place where it would get stuck if she was dug up and moved? I'll run it and compare it to the other soil samples we took, as well as the online database and see if I get any hits."

"Yeah. But why would they move her body?"

Katie shrugged. "I don't know. Maybe they didn't have a choice. Someone got too close, or an animal dug her up, perhaps."

He frowned. "Maybe. I'll get you that sample. Good work."

"Thanks. Are you two about done? It's eight-thirty."

"You don't have to stay."

She cast a quick look around him at Amanda, who was focused on the body. She had a magnifying glass in her hand, peering through it at the young girl's right humerus. "I wanted to talk to you," she said, keeping her voice quiet.

Heat licked his eyes, and she shivered. Katie bit her lip.

"Not just about that."

He nodded. "We'll be done soon. I'm not staying much longer, and it's my lab, so she's leaving, too, whether she wants to or not. The bones will still be here tomorrow. The bad guys are in custody, so it's not like we're racing against a clock to find them." He touched her shoulder. "Give me a few minutes and we'll close things up for the day."

"Okay."

He walked back over to the autopsy table and pulled on fresh gloves. He turned the victim's head to reveal the mandible joint. Using a swab, he teased out the compacted earth into a dish.

Katie came over and took the sample from him and put a lid on it. "I'll run it first thing in the morning."

Amanda frowned. "Why not now?"

"Because it's time to go home," Alex replied.

"What? We're not done."

Alex removed his gloves. "We are for tonight. It's late, Mandy. We all need to get some rest."

She spun the magnifying glass in her hand as she regarded

him. "It's not that late. We can still put another couple hours in."

Katie's eyes bulged, and she glanced at Alex. His brows rose and he crossed his arms.

"I'm not staying until nearly eleven o'clock. We've put in a full day—more than that, actually. Why are you so obsessed with this case?"

Amanda huffed and laid the magnifying glass down with a careful control but kept hold of the tweezers in her other hand. "I'm not. I just don't see the point in wasting time that could be used working."

"How about dinner? Or letting your mind rest by reading a book or watching TV?"

She waved a hand. "My mind is fine. And I'll grab a protein bar when I get back to the B&B."

He shook his head. "Katie's right. Something's up with you. Granted, I've never worked with you other than a brief consultation here and there, but this isn't like you. If you can't come clean, I'm afraid I'm going to have to call in another forensic anthropologist to assist us."

Her eyes widened, and Katie noted a hint of fear cross her face before she masked her expression.

"You can't do that, Alex. I have to be on this case."

"Why?"

"I just do. Can we leave it at that?"

"No." He sighed and put his hands on his hips. "Look, we're all tired. Take the night and think about things. We'll talk in the morning."

She stared at him for a moment, gauging how serious he was. Katie knew he meant what he said. He had that same look he gave her when she changed things in the lab, and he demanded she change them back. She'd learned the hard way she had to compromise, or he would fix it for her, and she wouldn't like it. Her large sample storage was now three floors above them in an empty office. Any time she wanted to run tests on one of those items, she either had to tote her equipment up there or find a cart and get the evidence back to the lab long enough to do what she needed. He still refused to let her bring the storage area back down to the lab.

Amanda's mouth flattened, and she tossed the tweezers onto a tray. They clanked against the other instruments. "Fine." She ripped off her gloves and gown, thrusting them into the trash can on her way out the door.

"You think she'll tell us what's going on?" Katie asked as the door swished shut.

He pinched the bridge of his nose, sighing. "If she really wants to stay on the case, she will." He dropped his hand. "Help me put our victim away, would you?"

Together, they made quick work of putting the Jane Doe back in her slot and disposing of the instruments used in her examination. Once they had everything squared away, they bade the night shift staff goodnight—with a warning to keep an eye out for Dr. Pressley should she decide to return—and headed for the parking lot.

Her stomach growled as they walked outside, reminding her she hadn't eaten. She thought about the leftover pizza in her fridge and cast a look at Alex from the corner of her eye. Would it be wise to ask him to come over after what happened yesterday?

Lost in thought, she tripped over the curb. As she lurched to the side, the car window in front of her shattered with the crack of a gun, the bullet missing her by a hair. She shrieked and dropped to the ground.

"Katie!"

Another bullet pinged off the car, digging into the asphalt inches from her. She let out another surprised shout. "Alex!"

Strong hands wrapped around her arms and pulled her behind another vehicle. The window shattered over their heads.

"Who's shooting at us?"

He wrapped her in his arms and hunched over her. "I don't know."

She clutched him as two more shots rang out. Tires squealed, then she heard people yelling as they ran out of the hospital and the police station next door to investigate.

He eased his hold on her, rising slightly to peek over the car. "I think it's safe now. Whoever it was drove off." He stood, pulling her up, but kept his arms around her. "Are you all right?"

Hands shaking, she brushed her hair back from her face. "I think so. Are you?"

He nodded.

The sound of boots on the pavement made them turn. They saw Deputy Reeves approaching.

"Dr. Randall? Ms. Mitchum? Are you two okay?"

Alex nodded. "We're fine."

"What happened?"

"Someone shot at us. But I didn't get a look at the shooter." He looked down at Katie. "Did you?"

She shook her head. "No. All I saw was glass flying."

"Same here." He glanced at the deputy. "Did anyone see the car? We heard tires squealing."

"I'm not sure. We'll check the security footage. Why would someone want to shoot you two?"

"I'm guessing it has something to do with the Paulson case," Katie said. Her eyes met Alex's, and she telegraphed who she thought was involved.

He frowned, catching her meaning. "No. She wouldn't. What would taking the two of us out accomplish?"

"Well, we did give her an ultimatum. Maybe she decided

she doesn't want to tell us why she's so obsessed and thinks removing us will keep her on the case."

Alex let go of her then to pace away several steps and rake his hands through his hair. "It just doesn't make any sense."

Reeves stepped forward. "What doesn't make sense? Who are you talking about?"

"Dr. Pressley," Katie said.

"The forensic anthropologist working with you?"

She nodded. "Yeah. We need to talk to the sheriff."

"He's probably on his way. I imagine Wilder called him the moment she heard the shots."

Katie sighed. Her stomach growled again. Looked like her pizza was going to have to wait.

The door to the conference room in the police station opened, and Katie glanced over to see Seb and Jace walk through. Seb carried a box, two plates, and two plastic forks, which he set on the table in front of them, then flipped open the lid.

"London sent some munchies," he said, sitting down.

Katie hooked a finger in the box and pulled it closer. She was starving. Two giant cinnamon rolls covered in cream cheese icing greeted her. Her mouth watered. She picked up a fork and stabbed one, lifting it out onto a plate before pushing the box toward Alex.

She bit into her roll and moaned as the flavors exploded on her tongue.

"Oh my God," Alex muttered around a mouthful of the sweet treat. "Tell your wife thank you. This is amazing. We haven't eaten since lunch."

"I figured. Now, what can you tell us about what happened?"

"I think it was Dr. Pressley," Katie said.

"You mentioned this morning you thought she was up to something," Seb said. "Did she do something else?"

"She's been very focused on the female victims, one in particular, for some reason. And this evening, she didn't want to leave, even though it was going on nine o'clock. She pressed us to stay, and Alex asked her why she was so obsessed with the case. She said she wasn't, but we both knew it was a lie, and he called her on it."

"I told her if she didn't come clean about why she was acting so out of character, I was going to call in a different forensic anthropologist. She got pissed and stormed out," Alex finished.

"Do you think she would shoot at you?" Jace asked.

Alex shrugged. "The Mandy I know wouldn't. But she's also not herself. I don't know what's going on with her."

The conference room door opened, and Deputy Reeves walked in, carrying a laptop.

"Here's the security footage, Sheriff." He handed Seb the computer and left.

Seb set the laptop on the table so they could all see it, then pressed play. The camera was mounted above the hospital's lobby doors and looked out over the parking lot. Katie watched as she and Alex exited the hospital. As they entered the lot, she tripped over the curb and the window of the car in front of her exploded.

Katie's head swam and her breathing kicked up as she realized if she hadn't tripped, that bullet would have hit her square in the back.

Seb paused the video as she pushed away from the table to hang her head between her knees. Alex's hand landed in the middle of her back.

"Hey, you okay?"

She made a noise in the back of her throat that wasn't really an answer, focusing instead on her breathing and the feel of his hand running along her spine so she didn't pass out. Seb and Jace stood, and she heard the door open. Seb's boots came into view, then his hands and chest as he crouched in front of her.

"Katie? Hey, you're okay." His voice was low and soft. "Just breathe. Look up at me and breathe."

She pushed up to rest her elbows on her knees and looked at him. He took her hands and held her gaze, breathing with her. Alex continued to run his hand up and down her back. It created a warm buzz that helped bring her out of her panicked state.

Inhaling a deeper breath, she blew it out and pulled her hands from Seb's. "I'm okay now."

He gave her a long look, then a brief nod before he stood. Jace came back into the room with a bottle of water. She took it from him, twisting off the top and taking a deep gulp.

"Are you sure you're okay?" Alex asked. He'd stopped rubbing her spine, but his hand remained on her back.

She turned to him and nodded. "Yeah. Seeing the footage —I didn't realize how close I came to being shot. If I hadn't tripped—" She broke off again, swallowing around the lump in her throat.

His hand curled over her shoulder, and he squeezed. She reached up and covered it with her free hand, offering him a tremulous smile before looking at Seb and Jace.

"I'm better now. You can continue with the video."

"You're sure?"

She nodded.

"Okay." Seb pressed play.

Katie stared at the screen and tried to watch it with the same detached eye she used when she watched footage from other crime scenes. Now they were behind a parked car. At the edge of the screen, she saw a muzzle flash from the driver's side window of a dark-colored SUV.

"Either of you recognize the car?" Seb asked.

"It kind of looks like the one Amanda drove," she remarked. "Although I can't tell if there's a university logo on it. It's angled wrong."

Alex dropped his head into his hands. "She's right. It does. I just can't believe she'd do such a thing." He looked up at Seb. "Can you call London and find out if she's back at the inn? That might answer our question about whether she was involved."

"Sure." Seb took out his phone and called his wife. They quickly learned Amanda had not returned. London promised to call if she did.

"This still doesn't make sense. Why would she try to kill Katie?" Alex asked.

"Well, there was strife between you two, right?" Jace said.

Katie nodded. "Yeah, but nothing I would expect someone to shoot me over. If anyone has a right to be the angrier party, it's me, because she basically called me a Luddite."

Alex waved a hand. "Whatever this is about—and even if Amanda's responsible—it's not because she dislikes Katie. It has to do with this case. One of those bodies has a secret someone doesn't want us to figure out."

"I agree," Seb said. "Which means digging into Amanda Pressley's background just became priority number one."

Katie stepped out of her bedroom, praying Alex would be up and dressed. When they left the police station last night, he insisted on coming home with her. She tried to tell him she would be fine, but he'd given her that same look he gave her when she wanted to put something somewhere in the lab he didn't want it. She knew there was no budging him when he had that look, and she was too tired to put up a fight. If he wanted to stretch his six-foot-three-inch frame out on her couch, let him.

But now, in the light of day, she regretted not pushing back. She wasn't ready to be faced with fresh out of bed, sexy Alex. The one who still had stubble on his jaw and maybe wasn't wearing a shirt.

Taking a deep breath, she rounded the corner from the hallway and braced herself. The couch was empty. She sniffed, smelling coffee, and walked through the living room to the kitchen. Alex stood at the counter, drinking a mug of coffee, his phone in his hand. He looked up from scrolling and smiled when she entered.

"Hey. I hope you don't mind. I made coffee and helped myself to a protein bar and a yogurt. We need to leave a little earlier than you normally would so I can go home and change."

She frowned as she took in his rumpled state. "Why didn't you just go home when you woke up? You followed me here last night."

"I know, but I'm not leaving you alone."

"Alex—"

He held up a hand. "Someone tried to shoot you. I know I'm not much protection since I'm not armed, but I'm at least another set of eyes and possibly a deterrent. Can we please not argue about this?"

She narrowed her eyes at him. "Fine. But only because I don't want to be late for work." She walked over to the coffeemaker and poured some of the dark brew into a travel mug, and snapped a lid on it. Moving to the fridge, she opened the freezer and took out a foil-wrapped breakfast burrito and tossed it in her lunch bag alongside a protein drink and a pre-made peanut butter and jelly sandwich. She zipped it closed and looked up to find a bemused expression on his face.

"What?"

"You eat like a grad student."

"I *am* a grad student."

He scoffed. "Hardly. Ph.D.'s are different. Especially when you already have a grown-up job." He pushed away from the counter, dumping the last of his coffee in the sink. "If you're ready, let's go."

She picked up her bag and followed him to the garage door where they left their shoes and coats when they came in the night before. In the garage, he pushed the button on the wall to open the overhead door, then paused and looked back.

"You should just ride with me. Unless Seb figures this out today, I'm coming back here tonight."

She looked at him over the top of her glasses.

"Don't give me that look. We had this discussion just a minute ago." He took her hand and pulled her toward the open door.

"Alex!" She huffed and lengthened her stride to keep up with him, pausing only long enough to hit the button just inside the door to close it.

He stopped beside the passenger door of his SUV, spinning around to face her. "I know I'm being overbearing, but —" He broke off and glanced away a moment, pressing his lips together before continuing. "You aren't the only one who was rattled by that video. Let me watch out for you? Please?" His voice dropped to a rough whisper.

Her shoulders fell. *Dammit.* "Fine." She stepped around him to open the door, ignoring the smile blooming over his handsome face. Sinking into the seat, she set her coffee mug in the cup holder, then put her lunch bag and purse at her feet before fastening her seatbelt as he climbed in beside her.

He started the car, then turned to her. When he opened his mouth to speak, she held up a hand.

"Don't. Just drive."

"Make yourself comfortable," Alex said, as they entered his house. "I'll be quick."

Katie nodded and took off her coat, laying it on the island in his kitchen. He left his coat next to hers, then hurried out to go take a shower and change.

Once he was gone, she looked around. This place was *nice*. He lived in an upscale neighborhood near the edge of town. His house was a craftsman-style, the exterior a mix of stone and gray siding. In the kitchen, where they'd entered from the garage, smoky granite counters topped natural wood cabinets. Clay-colored slate tile floors completed the look.

She wandered out to the main living space and couldn't stop her quick intake of breath as she got a look through the wall of windows at the back of the house where the roof came to a peak. The neighborhood was hilly, and Alex's house sat on a corner overlooking the valley. The morning sun sparkled on the frost left in the grass, and the mountains cast deep shadows on the landscape. It was beautiful.

Taking a reluctant step away from the window and the urge to go out onto the deck, she turned to peruse the rest of the room. High ceilings gave way to pine rafters and a balcony for the second floor. She could see a couple of doors from where she stood and assumed they led to bedrooms. A hallway cut to her left, and she saw several more doors. In the great room, large brown leather furniture dominated the space. A colorful geometric print rug in teals and oranges covered the floor of the sitting area. A large screen television was mounted on the wall above a stone fireplace.

Katie sank onto the couch, taking in the soft leather and the view beyond the windows. She wouldn't mind waking up to this. Hot coffee on the deck as the world woke up around her. She'd never want to leave.

But that was such a fanciful notion, she couldn't help but laugh out loud at herself. She and Alex may have shared one hell of a kiss, but it was a far cry from her moving in. If any two people were mismatched, it was them.

Spotting a wall of family pictures across the room, she got up and wandered over. The first one she looked at was a photo of a recent Christmas gathering. Alex stood next to an older version of himself. A third man stood on his other side. Katie guessed it was probably the brother-in-law. In front of the men stood two women, one young, one older. They sported matching smiles and the older woman held a baby dressed in a velvet red dress with a green headband on her bald head. Two boys who looked to be around eight and four stood in front of the women in matching red and black plaid shirts.

Another photograph was of Alex, the younger woman, and the older couple at what looked like his med school graduation. He had on a black graduation gown with the doctoral hood. A third picture was at the younger woman's wedding. More pictures of the children at various ages filled out the grouping. In each of them, the child sported a huge, cheerful smile. Katie couldn't help but smile back. They were adorable.

Turning away from the pictures, she stepped over to his bookshelves and tipped her head to read the titles. He liked suspense thrillers with a smattering of epic fantasy. There were also shelves full of medical texts, which she expected.

Noise from the hallway drew her attention. She glanced back to see Alex coming into the living room, buttoning another flannel shirt over a long-sleeved black tee. His dark hair was damp, shining in the overhead light.

"That *was* quick." She did her best to keep her eyes on his face and not let them stray to where he tucked the tails of his shirt into his pants.

"Took me longer to shave than anything else. Just let me grab something for lunch and we can go."

She followed him to the kitchen and shrugged back into her coat as he started coffee brewing while he made himself a sandwich. As the brewer sputtered the last of the coffee into his travel mug, he plucked a banana from the bunch on the counter. He put the food into a brown paper lunch sack, then put his coat on. Katie turned and headed for the garage, Alex right behind her.

The drive to the hospital was short, and he soon pulled into the doctors' lot. They got out and walked inside.

"Do you think Amanda will be here?" she asked as Alex punched the button to call the elevator.

He shrugged. "Maybe. I didn't see either of the university's SUVs in the lot when we drove in."

She checked her watch. "We're a little early, even with the pit stop at your house."

The elevator dinged, and the doors swished open. They stepped inside and she pushed the button for their floor. The doors closed, and they descended a floor to the laboratory level.

Katie stepped off and went to her desk while Alex headed for his office. She stowed her things in her desk, then unlocked the evidence cabinet and picked up the dirt sample from the Jane Doe last night. She would get it started while she waited on everyone else to arrive. The techs who remained behind could finish it once she left with the team to retrieve the last two bodies.

As she worked, the rest of her team filtered in. By the time she had the gas chromatograph up and running, they were all present and ready to go. She gave instructions to one of the techs remaining at the lab, then led the rest outside to the van. Amanda was nowhere to be found. Her team was outside waiting, though.

She walked up to the senior technician, Dave. "Where's your boss?"

He frowned. "She's not here?"

Katie motioned around them. "I don't see her, and she wasn't inside."

Dave's frown deepened. "Dammit. I was hoping she just worked late and went in early."

"So, she never came back to the inn last night?"

"Not unless she slipped in and out while we were all in bed. I never saw her."

"Is it normal for her to work so late?"

He shrugged. "Sometimes. But if she's not here, I don't know where she is."

Alex walked up then. "Did I hear you right? Amanda's missing?"

Dave nodded.

Katie glanced up at Alex, communicating silently. Things didn't look good for Dr. Pressley.

He held her gaze a moment before looking back at Dave. "Can you guys work without her?"

The older man frowned. "Well, I guess. We don't usually, at least not in the field, but I suppose we could." He gave them a perplexed frown. "Aren't you concerned about what happened to her?"

"Of course we are," Alex replied. "There was an—incident last night we think she might be involved in. The police are handling it. In the meantime, we still have a job to do. Let's get on the road."

Dave pursed his lips, curiosity shining bright in his eyes along with a healthy dose of concern for his boss, but he nodded. "Okay."

As he walked away, Katie turned and held out the van keys to Alex.

He took them with a smile, and they headed for the vehicle.

"This is nuts," he said. "I don't want to believe it was her who shot at us, but her disappearance does lend some credence to that theory."

"Yeah. We'll just have to wait and see what happens. I'm sure Seb has his deputies hard at work trying to locate her."

Alex's brow dipped in thought. "Yeah."

FIVE

The door to the path lab swished open, and Alex looked up to see Seb walk in.

"Hey. What's up?"

Seb glanced at the autopsy table where Alex worked on victim number four, an approximately fourteen-year-old girl, then up at the older man standing across the table from him.

"You must be Dr. White. I'm Sheriff Sebastian Archer."

The older man smiled and offered him a wave of a gloved hand. "Nice to meet you. I'm sorry it's under these circumstances."

"Me too."

"Do you have any news on Amanda?"

Alex wanted to know that too. He'd placed a call to her boss, Dr. Amos White, this morning on the way to the Paulsons' and informed him of what was going on, then asked if he could come down and fill Amanda's shoes to keep the investigation on track.

"Actually, I might. We were working under the assumption that she had something to do with the shooting last night, but we've gathered more surveillance footage since, and we went further back. Someone was waiting on Amanda when she left yesterday. The shots came from her car, but she didn't do the shooting. There were two men in a black SUV. One hit her over the head and stuffed her into the back of their car. The second one was leaving in her SUV when you guys entered the parking lot."

"My God! Do you think she's still alive?" Amos asked, echoing Alex's thoughts.

Seb shrugged. "Not sure. The blow didn't look hard enough to kill her. And if they wanted her dead, I would think they'd have just shot her like they tried to do with Alex and Katie."

"But why would they need her and not us?" Alex asked.

"Don't know. I put a BOLO out on both SUVs. One of the cameras caught the license plate on the black SUV, but it came back stolen out of Denver. We'll have to see what shakes out. In the meantime, Alex, you and Katie need to be careful. You probably should, too, Dr. White. Anyone involved in this case could be a target. The Paulsons had some high-profile clients, and any one of them could be out to stop us from uncovering something damning."

"Well, I'm staying under your roof, I believe?"

Seb nodded.

"I should be well looked after, then."

"Katie will be staying with me," Alex said, making the decision right there. She'd probably rant and rave at him, but he didn't care. "I spent the night at her place last night, but my house has an alarm system."

Seb grinned. "How'd that go?"

The memory of that kiss they shared the other night flooded his mind, and his body stirred. He shoved the thought away and lifted one shoulder. "Better than expected."

Seb's brow quirked. "Hmm. Good. Where is she, anyway?"

"Upstairs in large storage. She took our victims' clothes up there."

"Did they yield anything useful?"

"Not sure yet. She's running tests."

"Okay." He rapped his knuckles on the stainless-steel table. "I better head out and let you two finish up. Keep me updated."

"You do the same," Alex said.

"Yep. Call if you need me." Seb turned and left with a wave.

"Such strange business, these attacks," Amos commented, turning back to the body. "And all over these poor children."

"Yeah, well, someone did some awful things to these kids and doesn't want it to get out."

Dr. White's head bobbed. "True. I just hope your friend can find the person responsible—and Amanda—before something worse happens."

So did Alex. Forensics wasn't supposed to be a dangerous job.

Katie flipped over in her borrowed bed, trying to find a comfortable position. The bed was nice, but her mind wouldn't shut off. Too much had happened in the last twenty-four hours.

She sighed and sat up. This was ridiculous. Shoving off the covers, she got out of bed and crept downstairs on light feet. She snagged the throw off the couch and opened the sliding door to the deck off the living room. Outside, she wrapped the afghan around herself and sank into one of the deck chairs.

The moon was bright overhead, turning the frosty grass to silver. Her breath puffed white in front of her face, and she stared out over the quiet valley. She loved Alex's house. Even though they were still in town, it was so peaceful here.

She hadn't been happy to come home with him, though. It didn't matter that it was the prudent thing to do. Alex Randall was dangerous to her peace of mind. He was a large part of the reason she couldn't sleep.

Damn man...

Why couldn't he be a troll with a scraggly beard, crooked yellow teeth, and a potbelly? Better yet, why did she have to be attracted to older men? Weren't women her age supposed to want the young, virile ones? Although she couldn't say Alex *wasn't* virile.

A vision of him in his lumberjack clothes floated through her head. She never thought plaid could be so sexy.

Katie closed her eyes and leaned her head back in the chair. It didn't matter how attractive she found him. They would never amount to anything. She wasn't his type. She didn't know why he kissed her or told her she was beautiful. They were polar opposites. A polished, sophisticated woman like Amanda Pressley was more his speed.

The door slid open behind her with a soft swish. She opened her eyes and glanced back to see Alex standing in the doorway in a pair of lounge pants and a gray t-shirt.

"What are you doing out here? It's the middle of the night." His sleep-roughened voice rolled over her like fine whiskey.

She shrugged and huddled deeper into her blanket, looking back out over the valley. "I couldn't sleep."

There was a long pause—long enough she thought he went back to bed—before he sank into the seat beside her, another blanket wrapped around his shoulders.

"Why can't you sleep?"

Katie couldn't stop the laugh that bubbled past her lips. "You really have to ask?"

A sardonic smile tilted his mouth. "True. But I'd have thought it would have been worse last night."

"Yeah, well, I was in my own bed last night."

He sighed. "I'm sorry. I know I kind of railroaded you into coming here, but my place is safer."

She waved her fingers at him from where they were curled over the edge of the blanket. "I know. And I'm not really upset. At least, not at that. It's more the situation itself that has me angry. I mean, this case just doesn't want to behave normally, you know? Just when we think we have it figured out, it sends something else at us. First, it was Ryan Marsters. Then, Judge Brandt. Now, Amanda's been kidnapped. Why doesn't it want to die?"

Alex was silent for a moment. "I think this case has much larger implications than we imagined. April Stillwater did say her husband had some powerful friends. It stands to reason there are people outside of Silver Gap and Boone County who are involved. We're not that far from several large cities, including the state capital. There could be state representatives or even federal officials who partook of the Paulsons' services."

She let out a noise of disgust. "People are sick. And why is it that some of the most powerful ones are also the most deplorable?"

"Probably because many of them are a bit narcissistic and sociopathic. That type of personality doesn't mind stepping on some toes to get ahead. But it can have a downside, too, in the form of deviant behavior."

"Well, I'm looking forward to taking their deviant asses down."

He chuckled. "Me too."

A comfortable silence fell over them. Katie continued to stare out over the landscape, drinking in the peace. Her eyelids grew heavy, closing. Alex's chair creaked, and she heard him rise. Her mind drifting, she didn't open her eyes until she felt his arms slide under her knees and around her back. Then they flew open, meeting his. In the low light, they were midnight pools.

"What are you doing?"

"Putting you to bed." He straightened, lifting her from the chair with ease.

"I can walk, you know."

"Yep. But you looked comfortable. No use in you waking up more than you need to." He opened the door with one finger and stepped inside, closing it the same way, then throwing the lock. She punched in the alarm code, and he headed for the stairs.

Katie marveled at how nimbly he ascended them while carrying her, as though she weighed little more than the blanket. In her room, he laid her on the bed and removed the afghan, replacing it with the bedcovers. She tucked them under her chin and gazed up at him in the near-darkness. She could just make out his features in the moonlight.

He stroked her cheek with one finger.

Heat licked her veins, waking her up more than the trek through the house. "Alex." Her voice was a throaty whisper.

The muscles in his jaw ticked. He took a deep breath and stepped back. "Get some sleep."

As he turned to go, she snaked a hand out from under the blankets and grabbed his. He paused, looking down at her.

She took a shaky breath, not sure what she was doing. This was a bad idea.

"Don't go."

His muscles stiffened. "Katie—"

"I want you to stay. Just to sleep."

He hesitated, staring down at her.

"Please? I think we'll both sleep better." Just having him near calmed her mind. It might awaken other parts of her, but the restlessness plaguing her had disappeared when he sat down beside her on the deck. If he left, she was afraid it would all come right back.

He gave her a brief nod. She scooted over as he lifted the covers and climbed in beside her. Katie settled on her side, facing him. She toyed with the corner of her pillow while he got settled, suddenly nervous.

Nothing was going to happen, she reminded herself. Sleep. They were sleeping.

But the heat from his large frame was already warming the bed beneath the blankets. She wanted to scoot up against him and absorb it, even if she got burned in the process.

Katie scrunched her eyes closed and tried to picture a troll. The image of a garden gnome popped into her head instead, and she giggled.

"What's so funny?" His voice was groggy.

"Nothing." She giggled again as the gnome did a little jig.

She felt him roll onto his side.

"Not nothing. What's going on in that brilliant brain of yours?"

She opened her eyes to find him closer than she expected. Less than a foot separated their faces. Katie bit her lip and stared into his eyes in the dark.

"I was trying to distract myself."

"From what?"

"You."

A frown wrinkled his brow. "Me? Why?"

She rolled her eyes. "Again, you have to ask?"

His teeth flashed, bright in the darkness as he smiled. "I promise to stay on my side."

She sighed. "It doesn't help. But that's my problem to deal with. I'll go back to my gnome and leave you alone."

He huffed out a laugh. "Gnome? That's what you're using to distract yourself?"

"Well, it was supposed to be a troll. More specifically, you as a troll. But it morphed into a garden gnome." She lifted a shoulder.

His laughter filled the room, and she chuckled with him.

"What do I look like as a gnome?"

Katie giggled. "Rosy cheeks, pointy red hat. And you're wearing a plaid shirt with jeans and suspenders."

"Hmm... Sounds about right. Have you pictured yourself?"

She shook her head.

"I think you'd be very colorful. Tie-dye would suit you well."

"A tie-dye gnome?" She gave a small chuckle. "I'm not sure they make such a thing."

"Oh, they make all kinds."

"If you say so."

They fell silent, staring at each other. Tension ramped up in Katie's belly. Why did she have to laugh? She could be well on her way to sleep. Instead, she was struggling to remember why reaching out to feel the soft cotton of the t-shirt covering his broad chest was a bad idea.

She jerked as his fingers brushed the bare skin of her arm beneath her borrowed t-shirt. Tingles spread outward to race along her nerve endings and heat her flesh.

"Alex. We're supposed to sleep, remember?"

He inched closer. "Yeah."

Her head slid along the pillow toward him.

"I'm super tired. It's been a long couple days." His breath washed over her as he spoke, making her shiver.

"Yeah," she breathed, moving closer.

"So, we're agreed? We're going to go to sleep?"

The hand on her arm moved higher and covered more of her skin. She nodded in response to his question. "Yeah," she whispered again. Electricity sparked between them as only millimeters separated them now. Her eyes flicked down to his lips, then back. It was the last spark needed to ignite their desire. Alex closed the distance and fused his mouth to hers.

The need was quicker to punch her in the gut and flame brighter than the last time. Her body recognized his touch and wanted more.

His hand moved off her arm to curl over her shoulder and back, pulling her closer. She went willingly, throwing one bare leg over his hips. He skimmed his fingers down her back to wrap around her thigh. Katie rocked against him, sending spikes of fire through her body. His too, if his reaction was any indication. His grip tightened, and he groaned into her mouth. She cupped the side of his face, loving the rough feel of his beard stubble against her palm. It made her want to feel it elsewhere.

The blare of the house alarm broke them apart.

"What the hell?" Alex pulled away to look around.

"Why is your alarm going off?" Ardor effectively dashed, Katie sat up, scrambling off the bed behind Alex as he raced out of the room.

He ran downstairs to the door to view the main alarm panel by the front door. A light flashed red, and the display scrolled the location of the breach, but the direction of the breeze blowing through the room told her it was the sliding door.

As he turned off the alarm, she stood next to him and looked toward the windows. Shards of glass sparkled like diamonds on the hardwood floor. The icy breeze washed away any heat left from their encounter in the bedroom, and she shivered, crossing her arms over her chest.

A black shadow stepped out from the hallway. As she processed that it was a man dressed in black, he raised his arm. Wood splintered behind her at the same time she heard a loud pop from the silenced gun.

"Move!" Alex shoved her to the side, toward the stairs.

Glass shattered as a bullet went through a window. Katie shrieked as more thudded into the wall above her head as they beat a hasty retreat upstairs. Alex pushed her into her bedroom and to the other side of the bed, away from the door. He shoved her phone into her hands.

"Call for help."

She turned on the screen and hit the emergency call button as he crawled across the bed.

"Where are you going?" she asked, her whisper frantic.

"I left a gun in your nightstand. Just in case."

"What? You're armed?"

"Of course I'm armed. We live in bear and mountain lion country." He yanked open the drawer and withdrew a pistol.

Absently, she noted the larger caliber of the weapon and its suitability for protection from predators. Most of her attention was on the footsteps thundering up the staircase and the ringing in her ear as her phone call went through.

Alex jumped off the bed to take up a spot to the side of the door.

"Nine-one-one. What's your emergency?"

Katie jumped at the sound of the dispatcher's voice in her ear. *Jesus, I need to get a grip.*

She sucked in a breath and answered the woman on the other end of the line. "This is Katie Mitchum. I'm with Dr. Randall, and there's a man in his house with a gun."

"His alarm rang through to the police station a moment ago. There's a car on the way, ma'am. Is it just one man?"

"Yes." The word was barely audible. She could hear soft footsteps in the hallway. The doorknob rattled. Alex shifted his weight. She heard the safety click off as he raised his gun. Katie sank lower until all but her eyes were below the mattress. Spots danced in her vision as her breath came in short, shallow puffs. The door cracked open.

Police sirens split the night. The door stopped moving, and she heard the footsteps retreat in a hurry down the stairs.

She popped up above the mattress. "Is he gone?" she whispered.

Alex lowered his weapon. She could just make out his eyes glittering in the dark room.

"I think so," he whispered back. "Come on." He motioned her to come closer.

Rising, she hurried around, grabbing his arm.

"Hold on to my shirt in case I need my hands."

In answer, she twisted her hand in the bottom of his t-shirt. He nudged the door open and peered into the hallway.

"It's clear."

Together, they took cautious steps down the hall, keeping to the shadows near the wall so no one standing below could see them. When they reached the staircase, they paused, listening.

"I don't hear anything," she breathed into his ear.

"Me either. I think he left." He put the safety back on the gun, then took her hand and led her down the stairs, flipping on the overhead lights when they reached the bottom.

"Stay there. There's glass all over the floor." He stepped down, staying along the wall. The window next to the front door was shattered now, in addition to the sliding door.

"You're not wearing any shoes, either."

He didn't answer her, instead giving her a look that told her not to argue. He hurried past the radius of the glass and into the kitchen, then came back a moment later wearing a pair of tennis shoes and carrying her boots from earlier. She stuffed her feet into them and followed him away from the stairs to the door, where she could hear the sirens getting louder.

Alex tucked his weapon into his waistband at the small of his back and opened the front door as a squad car pulled into the driveway. It was the city police, she noted. The officer cut the siren, but left the lights on, and stepped out of his vehicle, then walked up the sidewalk.

"Dr. Randall?"

"Yes. Come in, officer."

"I'm Officer Danby." The man stepped over the threshold and let out a low whistle as he took in the damage. "Someone was either a poor shot, or you got lucky."

"It was dark," Alex replied. "And just so you know, I'm armed." He pointed to his back.

The officer's gaze sharpened, and he rested a hand on the butt of his gun. "Remove the gun slowly and hand it to me, please."

Alex did as asked.

"Did you shoot back?" Danby asked, checking the safety on Alex's gun. He tucked it into his belt.

"No. He surprised us when we came down to investigate and turn off the alarm. I grabbed that when we ran back upstairs. I never had to use it. He fled when he heard your siren."

Danby nodded and picked up the radio mic on his shoulder. "Dispatch, send additional units to my location, including K-9. Burglary suspect fled on foot."

"Copy, sending additional units."

The officer dropped the mic back in place and turned his attention on them. "What happened?"

"We were in bed and the alarm went off. We came downstairs to a broken slider."

"But no one was in the room?"

"No," Katie said. "He came out of the hallway after Alex turned off the alarm. I saw him right before he raised his gun and took a shot at us. It hit the wall behind me." She pointed at the hole in the wall to the left of the door. "We took off up the stairs, and he shot several more times." She motioned to the broken window and the holes in the wall leading up the staircase.

"Did either of you get a look at his face?"

Katie glanced at Alex, then they both turned to the deputy and shook their heads. "No. It was too dark."

"He was dressed in all black. He was white and about six-feet tall. That's all I can tell you."

"Slender? Muscular?"

They shared another look.

"Average," Katie said.

The front door opened again, admitting another officer. Seb was right behind him.

"Are you guys okay?"

"We're fine," Alex answered. "Shaken up, but unharmed."

"The K-9 is outside. Hopefully, we can track this guy down."

"I think he fled through the broken slider," Katie said. "I don't remember hearing the front door close." She hugged herself tighter, a fine shiver running through her. Now that the adrenaline was wearing off, she was starting to feel the chill from the broken windows.

"Okay. Officer, tell the K-9 where to begin searching, then help secure the scene. Because Ms. Mitchum is with our forensics department, I've called the neighboring county for assistance. They should have someone here within the hour."

"Yes, sir." The officer left.

Katie curled her toes inside her boots and bounced a little, trying to warm up. Alex noticed.

"Jesus, Katie, you must be freezing." He walked over to the couch and picked up the afghan she used earlier and wrapped it around her shoulders.

"Thank you." She curled her fingers over the edge and clutched it close, welcoming its warmth, then glanced at Seb. "So, what now? This was supposed to be the safest place for us. If he could get this close with Alex's alarm, my place would be a piece of cake."

"I thought about that on my way over here. You could come stay at the inn—"

"No." Katie cut him off. "I'm not putting London's business in danger. She went through that with Marsters. We're not doing it again."

"Yes, but the security is much better than it was then. Plus, most everyone around here knows I live there now."

"Doesn't matter. Pick a different place."

Seb frowned. "Okay. What about the Broken Bow? My house and Thomas's are vacant. Both have alarm systems."

"Don't your parents have the kids you found staying with them, though?" Alex said.

Seb nodded.

It was Alex's turn to frown. "I don't like the idea of bringing more danger to them. Especially since it seems to be connected to their case. We could just stay here. Not tonight, since the windows are broken, but we could get them boarded up tomorrow and then come back. I mean, what's the likelihood they'll strike here twice?"

"Better than you'd think," Seb said.

"But where else can we go, then?" Katie asked.

"What about a hotel?" Alex suggested. "Pueblo is an hour away. The commute would suck, but it's doable."

Seb sighed. "I guess that would work, if you two don't mind the drive."

"It's fine," Katie said.

Alex gave a quick nod. "We're agreed, then."

"Okay. I'll make the reservations just in case someone gets ahold of one of your credit cards." He gave a sudden grin. "Am I booking one room or two?"

Katie flushed to the roots of her hair and glanced at Alex. He stared at her, his eyes darkening, then glanced at Seb.

"One. But with two beds."

Seb laughed. "If you say so." He took out his phone. "Go get dressed and pack. We'll swing by Katie's place to get some of her things on the way to Pueblo."

Face still flaming, she scurried past him and Alex to go find her clothes. This situation just kept getting better and better.

Six

Smothering a yawn, Katie blinked to bring her computer screen back into focus. She picked up the tepid coffee on her desk and took a sip. Even a Big Gulp full of the stuff wouldn't be enough to wake her up today.

After Seb left them at a hotel in Pueblo, sleeping hadn't been a problem anymore. Katie had dropped onto one of the beds and passed out. But by that point, it was already after three, so she'd gotten only a couple hours of sleep before they had to be up to drive back to Silver Gap for work.

Her phone rang, and she picked it up, smothering another yawn. "Forensics. This is Katie."

"Hey, it's Jackie. Girl, you're never going to believe what I found."

Katie perked up at the sound of her friend and fellow criminologist's voice. Jackie Bollen worked for the adjacent county where Seb sent the evidence from Alex's house.

"What did you find?"

"Is that handsome M.E. there? He should hear this, too."

Katie glanced up, looking around the room. She didn't see Alex, but his door was open.

"Yeah. Hang on a second." She put her on hold, then transferred the call to Alex's line before dashing across the lab to his office.

He looked up, startled, as she flew through the door just as his phone rang.

"Answer that." She pointed at his phone and came around to stand beside him. "I just transferred it from my phone. It's Jackie with a report on your house."

He pressed the speakerphone button. "This is Dr. Randall."

"And me, Jackie," Katie said.

"Good. Okay, so, I ran the bullets we dug out of the walls and they came back as a match to *twelve* murders in the western United States."

"Twelve?" Alex turned to look up at Katie, who stared down at him with the same look of disbelief.

"Yeah. I couldn't believe it either, so I dug a little deeper. The cops in several of the cases think they were contract killings."

"He must not cost much. He can't aim worth shit, thankfully," Katie said.

Alex looked up at her again and arched a brow.

"What? It's true. He's tried to shoot us twice now and missed both times. With multiple shots."

He sighed, shaking his head, then turned back to the phone. "Did you uncover anything else?"

"Not yet. I just thought you guys should know what you're up against."

"We appreciate it. Thanks, Jackie." Katie leaned over Alex's shoulder and picked the receiver up, then replaced it to end the call.

He sat back, swiveling to face her. "Well."

"Yeah."

"I think we need to talk to Seb again."

"I agree." She gestured to the phone. "Call him."

Alex sighed and pursed his lips, but turned and picked up the receiver. He only got half the numbers entered before the lab doors opened and Seb walked in. Katie could tell by the set to his jaw and the wrinkle between his brows that Jackie called him first.

He made a beeline for Alex's office, spying them behind the desk. "We need to talk." He stepped inside and closed the door.

"We know," Alex said. "Jackie called us after she called you."

"I think it might be safest if we turn all this over to the FBI."

"You *were* FBI," Katie said.

"Emphasis on the past tense. I might have the investigative abilities, but I don't have the resources. Without Paulson's or Brandt's cooperation, we need those. Plus, I think the danger to you two will disappear with the bodies."

"What about Amanda?" Alex asked.

Seb shrugged. "Maybe they'll let her go if all our evidence goes to the feds."

"Or they'll kill her."

"This is ridiculous," Katie said. She moved around the desk toward Seb. "We just need to figure out what they're trying to hide. I have a feeling it has to do with the girl Amanda was paying so much attention to the other day. The one I thought had been moved. She's the key." She looked up at Seb, who blocked the door. "I need you to move so I can get back to work."

He just frowned down at her. "I'm serious, Katie. I think we need to let the feds handle this now."

She rolled her eyes and glanced back at Alex. "Back me up here. Let's go over that Jane Doe with a fine-toothed comb. There has to be something there."

Alex hesitated, his eyes moving between them, until he sighed and ran a hand through his hair. "Don't turn it over yet. Let us at least try."

Seb's mouth flattened. He stared at them a moment longer, his expression hard. "You get the weekend. If you don't have anything by Monday morning—or something else happens—I'm calling the FBI." He looked at Katie. "Agreed?"

She nodded. She could work with that. "Agreed."

"Okay. In the meantime, my deputies are now your best friends. One will be stationed with you at all times, even here in the hospital. Neither of you goes anywhere alone, even here. If one of you leaves the lab and then the other needs to leave as well, you have to wait on one of my deputies to get here to escort you."

"Seriously?" Katie crossed her arms and glared up at him. "We really need shadows?"

"Someone tried to shoot you. Twice. Yeah. You do."

She growled under her breath. Seb bent his knees to look into her eyes.

"You'll behave, yes? Because I can still take away the case if you won't follow my rules."

"She'll be good." Alex stood. "We'll be careful."

"Good. Gentry's sitting just outside the lab doors. I need to get back to the station. Call me if you need me." He turned to leave, but paused, looking back. "And let me know when you're ready to head for Pueblo."

They nodded, and he left with a wave. Katie frowned, watching his tall figure as he walked out of the lab. This sucked.

She knew how to make it better, though. Find out what the bad guys were so eager to hide.

"Come on." She looked at Alex. "Let's take another peek at that body."

Alex tried not to stare at Katie as she sat cross-legged on the bed. She munched on loaded nachos as she studied the open file in front of her. They'd worked several more hours before calling it a day. After stops for clothes and food, they checked into their hotel room. Katie locked herself in the bathroom to take a shower as soon as they walked inside. Now, she sat across from him in her miniscule pajama shorts and loose top. At least she had a sports bra on under the shirt. He could see the strap peeking out from the neckline, which shifted lower every time she reached for something. She was trying to kill him.

But two could play that game. He'd taken one look at her attire and excused himself to take a shower as well. When he returned to the main room, he wore only his navy blue lounge pants, deliberately leaving his t-shirt in his bag. It had been worth it to see her face. Twin pops of color brightened her cheeks, and those big hazel eyes of hers grew dark as she stared at his bare chest. She didn't take the bait, though. He knew she found him attractive. The feeling was mutual. But for some reason, she was reluctant to get involved.

She drove him nuts. A week ago, he would have said no way to a relationship, but something changed in the last few days. He found her sass invigorating now instead of annoying. He had a feeling their dinner the other night was to blame. Getting to know her better altered the way he viewed her, and he liked what he saw.

Cheese sauce from her nachos smeared on the corner of her mouth as she took another bite. Her tongue darted out to lick it away, and Alex stifled a groan. He shifted, bringing his knees up to hide his reaction to her. He needed a distraction.

"Let's go over what we know."

She looked up and sighed. "Okay. Where do you want to start?"

"The victim. White thinks she was about fifteen when she died, but can't really tell me how long she's been in the ground."

She frowned. "Based on the style of clothing she had on, I'd say she's been dead fifteen to twenty years."

"That makes sense. The Paulsons started their operation about twenty years ago. Maybe they pulled up stakes early on and were afraid to leave her body behind, so they moved her with them."

Katie shuddered. "Those two are sick." She pushed her nachos away. "I'll try some fluorescence techniques tomorrow and see if I can pull some style numbers off the tags in her clothes. I can cross-match them with the brand and maybe get a year they were produced."

He nodded. "I told Seb to go back ten years for his missing persons search, but I'll tell him to expand it another ten in the morning. What else did you notice?"

"There wasn't any blood on her clothes. Did you or White find anything to indicate cause of death?"

"No. She had some old fractures in several bones, but they all showed some degree of remodeling."

"Okay. Can you get me a sample of her femur? I'll run it for drugs. Unless the levels are off the charts, it won't tell us if that was the cause of death, but it can definitely tell us if they were involved. It can also tell us more about her. What kind of water she drank, nutrition—that sort of thing."

"How long will it take?"

She frowned. "It'll be Sunday before I can run tests on the sample. It has to soak in methanol for about eighteen hours first. But once that step is complete, drying and testing will only take an hour, maybe."

Alex closed his now empty to-go box and rested his arms over his bent knees. "We're cutting Seb's deadline really close."

"I know. But it can't be helped. The tests take time."

He sighed. "I wish Seb could get Paulson or Brandt to talk. Whoever they're covering for must scare them more than all the jail time they're facing." He dropped his legs and stood, picking up the remains of his dinner, then pointed at hers. "You done?"

She nodded, scrunching her nose, and handed it to him. He knew how she felt. His food sat like lead in his stomach. They should have picked different dinner conversation.

"I feel dirty now," she said, getting up to put the files away. "Like I need another shower."

Alex dropped the takeout boxes in the trash and looked back. She stood next to the desk with her arms wrapped around her middle. A tiny frown marred her face. His heart lurched at the sight. He hated seeing her upset.

"Hey." He walked over and put his hands on her biceps, running them lightly over her skin. "We're going to find out who she is and who's after us."

Her mouth pulled to the side, and she glanced up at him through her lashes. "I know. It still doesn't erase the disgust." She dropped her arms and tipped her head to look at him. "Why do some people have to be so twisted?"

He ran his hands up her arms and over her shoulders to cradle her head. His thumbs brushed her cheeks while his fingers threaded through her damp hair. "God only knows, honey. But that's why we do what we do. To stop them."

She brought her hands up to cover his and stared up at him with her pretty hazel eyes. Alex got caught in her gaze. He shifted his stance to bring her closer and leaned down. She watched him as he neared.

"If I kiss you again, I don't want to stop."

A fine tremor went through her at his words, and her

pupils dilated. In answer, she stretched up and sealed her mouth to his.

What the hell am I doing?

Katie slid her arms around Alex's neck and pressed herself against his naked chest. The damn man did this deliberately. Came out half-naked to force her to confront her feelings. With the stress of the case and the memory of how it felt to be in his embrace, she was a goner. She'd probably regret this when he decided she wasn't what he wanted in a long-term relationship, but right now she couldn't bring herself to care. He pushed all the right buttons and ticked all the correct boxes for what she found irresistible in a man.

His hands moved down her arms to grip her waist before sliding around, one hand on her back, the other kneading her butt. He took two steps forward, backing her up, and they toppled onto the bed. Her eyes rolled back until she could see her brain when his mouth left hers to trail along her neck and past the neckline of her top. That beard stubble felt so good!

She ran her fingers up his sides, loving the feel of muscle over bone. He sucked in a breath and pulled back, grabbing the hem of her shirt and pulling it over her head. Katie didn't wait for him to take off her bra. She whipped it over her head, tossing it to the floor, and reached for him again. He dodged her grip, though, to bend his head and take one nipple in his mouth.

Holy hell!

She clutched fistfuls of his hair and hung on as he sent her soaring up the peak.

Sensing she was losing control, he lifted his head. Mischief danced in his eyes.

"Like that, did you?"

"No. It sucked," she quipped, breathless. "Why'd you stop?"

He sat up. "I had other plans to send you over the edge the first time." He palmed her breasts, skating his hands down her torso to her hips. Snagging her pajama shorts and panties, he pulled them down her legs. His eyes turned a deep indigo as he focused on her now exposed core. Without thinking, her knees fell apart.

"Damn," he whispered and glanced up at her. "We need to make this last, because I only have one condom."

"I'm on the pill. And I'm clean. I made sure of that after my divorce."

A wicked smile crossed his face, and he stood, shucking his pants and boxer briefs. All the moisture left her mouth to flood south at the sight of him.

He noticed where she'd fixed her gaze, and his smile grew. "I'm glad we can have as much fun as we want, but I still have plans for you before we go that route."

Katie yelped as he grabbed her ankles and pulled her to the edge of the bed, kneeling in front of her. *Yes!* She tipped her head back and closed her eyes, anticipating the feel of his rough stubble on her sensitive flesh.

He didn't disappoint. Kissing his way down her inner thigh, his first touch to her core made her buck off the mattress. Alex wrapped his arms around her thighs and held her in place. Katie was helpless to do anything except grip the bedsheets as he sent her flying over the precipice with his evil mouth and eviler beard.

She didn't get a chance to come down before he stood and pushed her up the bed. Settling between her legs, he slid into her with one smooth stroke. She crossed her ankles around his waist and held on as he drove her back up the peak.

Heat coiled in her belly, slicking her skin with sweat. Their soft sighs and moans filled the small room, turning to shouts of pleasure as they toppled over the edge together.

Katie's bones dissolved as wave after wave of the most intense orgasm she'd ever had rolled over her. She melted into the bed and savored Alex's weight on top of her.

He groaned as he came down from his own high and rolled to the side. She shivered as the cool air hit her damp, heated skin. Alex tucked her into his side and drew the blankets up over them.

"Now we really need another shower," she said, her eyes drooping.

He chuckled and kissed the top of her head. "Not yet. I need a few minutes."

She raised her head to look at him. He had his eyes closed. "Who said I wanted you to join me?"

He raised one brow but didn't open his eyes. A smile quirked one corner of his mouth.

Katie giggled. "Okay. But I don't know how you're going to manage anything in there. It's not the most spacious area."

His smile grew. "You'll see."

Some of the starch returned to her bones at his words and the Cheshire-cat grin on his face. "Cocky bastard, aren't you?"

That made him open his eyes. Mischief sparkled in their depths. It was fun to poke the bear. He rolled onto his side, his hand sliding over her breast to pluck the nipple.

Her eyes fluttered closed and her lips parted on a sigh.

So much fun...

Seven

"Did you finish prepping your tests?" Alex walked up behind Katie and did his best not to lean into her. She had her hair twisted up into a bun with a pencil to keep it out of the way, exposing her neck. He wanted to bury his nose behind her ear and breathe her in.

She glanced back and smiled, her eyes lighting with desire as she took him in. "Yes. Why?"

"I'm ready to get out of here. How about we go find a rock face and do some climbing? The weather's great."

A frown dipped her eyebrows. "Now? We don't have too much daylight left. And what about this case?"

He shrugged. "We have several hours yet. It's only two. I have a bunch of camping gear in my garage. We could find a spot and stay out overnight. And we're playing a waiting game now until the tests are ready to run and you get information back on the victim's clothing. Dr. White and I finished our preliminary autopsies. He wants to do some more in-depth analysis of the bones, but that's all him. I don't do skeletons."

"He might need my help."

"Devin can handle it. Come on, Katie. We both need a break."

She stared at him for several moments before nodding. "Okay. Let me put these in the evidence locker and we can go."

Alex resisted the urge to do a fist pump. Work was the last thing he wanted to do today after last night. He wanted to get her alone and have a repeat. "I'll let Seb's deputy know." He stepped away to let her clean up her workstation and went to tell the deputy their plan. He'd likely protest, but Alex didn't care. They'd be in the middle of nowhere. It would be hard for someone to follow unnoticed.

He took out his phone, intending to bypass the deputy and go straight to the boss. The young man sitting outside the lab couldn't protest if his boss said it was okay.

Seb picked up on the third ring. "Hey, Alex. Something wrong?"

"No. Katie and I are cutting out. There's not much we can do until her tests are complete. We're going to head up into the mountains and do some climbing. Probably stay out overnight."

"You want to go camping? Now? My deputy does not want to have to listen to the two of you all night."

"How do you know that's what we'll be doing?"

"My deputies have eyes, Doc. Gentry reported the change in your relationship when he briefed me this morning. You weren't exactly discrete with the kiss you laid on her before you entered the hospital."

Alex smiled as he remembered. That *had* been nice. He knew once inside, they'd have to keep things professional, so he'd made sure the kiss would be enough to last them until they could leave. It kind of backfired on him, though. It just made him want more.

"The deputy can stay behind at the trailhead. If we make sure we aren't followed up there, we should be safe."

Seb sighed. Alex could picture him pinching his brow as he thought.

"Swing by the Broken Bow on your way up and get a sat phone. Your cell won't work in the mountains."

"Will do. Thanks, Seb, for not arguing."

"I get the need to get away. I do. Just watch your backs. Take your gun and don't get complacent. And leave your cell phones at home just in case they're being tracked."

Alex agreed and hung up. He hoped they weren't making a mistake, but he wouldn't let this lunatic dictate how he lived his life. He knew Katie felt the same. She'd fought the protective custody Seb put her in a few months ago when she had that thumb drive Tim Masterson and Jared Fetter thought they destroyed in the lab fire. She complied, but protested loudly. Alex knew if it had lasted much longer, she would have told Seb to take a hike.

He poked his head through the lab door and told the young deputy, named Reeves, what they were doing and that Seb had already approved. With a nod, Reeves acknowledged him. Alex went back into the lab to inform Amos of the plan.

The older man looked up as he approached the table where he worked on victim number five, a boy about thirteen years-old.

"Katie and I are leaving for the day. She's got some samples prepping, but they won't be ready to run until tomorrow. If you need anything, ask Devin for help."

"Taking a break, eh? I can't say I blame you. It's been a crazy few days for you two."

"Yeah. We're going climbing and camping overnight. Some peace and quiet will do us both good."

"Well, be careful. Will I be able to get a hold of you if I need to?"

Alex nodded. "We're taking a satellite phone. I don't know the number yet, but I'll text it to you once we stop and pick it up."

"Sounds good. Have fun."

Katie walked up with her purse in her hands. "I'm ready."

He smiled down at her. "Let me go lock my office."

After gathering his things, they bade the staff goodbye and left the lab. Reeves followed on their heels to the parking lot, where they climbed into Alex's SUV with the deputy behind the wheel. Alex gritted his teeth the entire drive—just like he had to and from Pueblo—but even he recognized it was smart to let the deputies drive. He and Katie weren't trained on defensive driving; the deputies were.

It didn't mean he liked it, though. Katie gripped his hand and did her best to distract him with conversation, knowing he was uncomfortable. He kept his eyes on her and not out the windows at the passing scenery. They made a couple quick stops to get their climbing and camping gear and to change, then another at the Broken Bow for the sat phone. Seb's mom loaded them up with extra food for them and the deputy. Alex's mouth watered when he caught sight of the fried chicken.

Within a couple hours of leaving the lab, Reeves pulled into a parking lot at a trailhead near a decent climbing zone. There was another spot Alex liked more, but it was much more remote than this location. With the afternoon waning, they didn't have time to hike to it and still have enough daylight to climb.

Reeves handed them their packs, concern etched onto his young face. "You sure you want to do this?"

Alex glanced at Katie, whose emphatic nod made him smile.

"We're sure," she said, taking her climbing gear from the back of the SUV.

Removing his own gear, Alex closed the hatch. "We'll be fine, deputy. No one but a select few know where we are, and you made sure we weren't followed. Enjoy my ergonomic leather seats and premium sound system. We'll see you in the morning."

Reeves sighed. "It is considerably nicer than the police cruiser." His expression sobered. "Just watch your backs. If something seems even the tiniest bit off, call me."

Alex nodded, buckling his pack straps around his waist. "We will." He looked at Katie. "You ready?"

"Yep." She clicked her buckle together. "Let's go."

They waved at Reeves and set off down the trail. It was about a mile to the rock face over hilly terrain. Thankfully, the path was well-traveled, so they weren't picking their way through thick undergrowth. They kept a quick pace and reached the climbing zone in just over half an hour.

After tying up their camping supplies and food, they began unpacking climbing equipment, readying ropes and pulleys. Once they had things set up the way they liked, they checked each other's gear, then switched out their shoes and put on their helmets. Alex chalked his hands and studied the cliff, mapping a path to the top.

Katie tossed him a grin and hopped onto the rock, clinging to it like a monkey. He admired the play of her muscles as she scampered higher before following her.

For the next couple hours, they picked their way up the rock face. With every foot higher, Alex felt his mind relax. It had been too long since he'd been away from the office. He loved what he did, but constantly immersing himself in the dirtier aspects of human nature wasn't healthy. He vowed to take more time away.

Katie swung sideways on the cliff to reach another hand-hold, drawing his eyes. Now that he had her in his life, time off sounded much more appealing.

"You know, we wrap this case up and we should consider taking some time off. More than just an afternoon."

She paused and looked over her shoulder at him, resting for a moment. "I wish I could. Until my dissertation is done, this is the most I can hope for. But you have fun."

He frowned. "I didn't mean I wanted to go alone."

"Oh. Well, I'm sure you could find someone to go with you. Maybe Seb or Jace. Or Amanda, if she ever shows up and isn't actually a psycho." She looked up and pushed herself higher with one leg to reach for her next handhold.

"That's not what I meant, either."

She sighed and glanced down again. "What did you mean, then?"

He stared up at her for several seconds. "You. I want to go with you. How did that not occur to you?"

She shrugged and started climbing again. "Why would it? This thing between us is fun, but do you really see it going anywhere?"

Did he—what the fuck was she talking about? He ran his eyes over the rock above him and made a series of quick moves until he was at her level.

"Hold up a second. Why do you think we couldn't have anything serious? I don't know about you, but last night was like no other."

"Well, yeah, but come on, Alex. We aren't exactly suited."

"How so? We're both smart, have similar interests, and we work in related fields. I'd say that's a pretty good basis for a relationship."

"Do we have to talk about this while we're hanging off the side of a mountain?"

"Yes. You're a captive audience. Answer the question."

She shifted her weight to her other foot. "Look at me, then look at yourself. There's a picture of you in the dictionary next to the word 'clean-cut.' I'm not even close to that. I like tattoos and punk rock music. My hair is vibrant more often than not, and I'm not exactly known for my demure nature."

"I don't care about any of that stuff. It's all just packaging. You're beautiful no matter what color your hair is or what's on your skin. And I admit, you drive me insane some days, but I enjoy sparring with you. Your mind fascinates me. Life is never dull with you in it. I love that."

She stared back at him with wide eyes. "What? No. You're ready to throttle me on a daily basis."

"At first, yes. Then it was just fun to get a rise out of you. Your eyes turn this silver color and you puff up like an angry peacock. It's cute."

She threw her head back and laughed. "That's what a girl wants to hear. Being compared to a peacock."

He chuckled. "Why not? They're stunning creatures. My point is, I like you. More every day. I don't want this to be a fling, Katie. I thought that before we had sex. Last night just solidified my feelings."

She turned and stared at the rock in front of her. Alex could see her contemplating his words. Her expression ran the gamut from thoughtful to disbelief before settling on cautious hope. She looked at him again.

"I want to believe you, but I don't have the best instincts about men. My ex seemed like a great guy until he wasn't. I don't want to fall for you and have you stomp all over my heart. I think you could do a million times more damage to it than Jonas ever did."

Alex cursed his decision to have this conversation on the side of the mountain. He wanted to touch her. So badly. But they were stuck where they were until they reached the top.

"Katie, I know things have been rocky since you moved into the lab, but I respect you. Both as a colleague and as a woman. I want to see where we can go with this."

She bit her lip, glancing away a moment. "But what

happens the first time we go to some fancy doctor function and your colleagues look at me like I'm the help? And look at you like you're slumming it?"

"They can go fuck themselves. The people who matter won't care about how you look. They will appreciate you for you, just like I do. And the people who do care about how you look don't matter. Besides. Pretty soon, you're going to have the same moniker. I can't wait to see their stuffy faces when you're introduced as Dr. Mitchum."

That drew a smile, and she tipped her head. "I guess that will be a bit amusing."

"Very." He motioned to the top of the cliff with his head. They only had fifty feet to go. "Come on. Let's finish this climb. My toes are starting to feel it." So were his fingers. It had been far too long since he'd done this sort of thing.

They finished their climb, both lost in thought and concentrating on their movements. Alex's muscles burned as he pulled himself onto the top of the ridge. Katie's head rose above the edge, and he held out a hand to her, hauling her over. They flopped together on the ground, breathing hard.

"Oh my God," she breathed. "My muscles hate me right now."

He chuckled. "I was just thinking the same thing. We need to do this more often."

"Winter's coming." Her chest heaved. "We'd have to make regular trips into Pueblo or Colorado Springs to the gym to keep up with it."

Alex groaned and sat up. "Might be worth it. Damn. I didn't realize I was so out of shape."

She scoffed and sat up next to him. "Whatever. I saw you naked. You don't have anything to worry about."

He gave her a wicked grin. "Muscles used for running are different from those for rock climbing. My calves are on fire."

"Mine too." She brought her knees up and rested her chin on them, staring out over the landscape below them.

The breeze blew over them, lifting Katie's brightly colored tresses to tease them over her shoulder. A few tendrils danced across her cheek. He reached out to brush them away. She turned to look at him.

"I know you're skeptical about us, but I'm not going anywhere. You're going to get sick of me before that happens."

A smile quirked her mouth. "That's a given."

He chuckled and tucked her hair behind her ear, leaning closer to press a gentle kiss to her lips. Pulling back, he tapped her nose. "Come on. Let's head down. I'm starving, and Jenny's chicken is calling my name."

"I want that cake she packed," Katie said, rising.

"Are you one of those women I just have to buy chocolate for and all is forgiven?" He anchored their rope to a tree.

One corner of her mouth lifted, and she gave him a side-eye glance. "Maybe."

"That's good to know." Alex stood at the edge of the cliff and walked backward over the edge.

She took up her position and followed him over. "If you're really bad, it's going to take more than a box of truffles to make it up to me."

He grinned. "Duly noted."

The chirp of a bird on the ground outside the tent and the gentle flutter of its wings as it shook the dust from its feathers roused Katie. Dim light greeted her as she opened her eyes. The sun was just coming up.

Warm and not ready to move yet, she snuggled deeper into Alex's side. Stretching an arm over his chest, she tangled her fingers in his chest hair, loving the crisp feel of it. He stirred beneath her, inhaling deep as he came awake. His eyes fluttered open, their sleepy blue depths taking her breath away. She was still in shock that this beautiful man wanted her. *Her.* The tattooed loudmouth who'd rather be stuck to the side of a mountain in a pair of stretchy shorts and a sports bra than in a sharp business suit and heels.

"Good morning." His low voice rumbled over her, raspy with sleep. Heat flooded her core.

She smiled at him. "Good morning."

He turned toward her, his free hand roaming over her hip to grab her butt. She swung her leg over his waist as his mouth came down on hers. They'd exhausted each other last night, but it didn't matter. She didn't think she'd ever get enough of him.

A moan broke free from her chest when he rolled his hips, teasing her with his hard length. She felt him smile against her neck.

The trill of the sat phone broke them apart. Alex cursed, while Katie dropped her head to his chest and groaned.

"That better be important."

"It probably is." He rolled away to pick it up.

She tucked the sleeping bag under her arms and sat up. "Who is it?"

He held up a finger and answered it. "Dr. Randall."

She watched a frown dip his brow.

"Hang on, slow down. Let me put you on speaker." He took the phone away from his ear and looked at her. "It's Devin. There's a problem at the lab." He punched the speakerphone button. "Go ahead, Devin."

Her assistant's voice filled the tent. "So, I just got here and someone ransacked the lab. All the evidence that was in here is now all over the floor. Including the bodies. And they're not just on the floor. Someone smashed them. There are thousands of bone fragments everywhere."

Katie groaned.

Alex's face turned red, and a vein pulsed in his forehead. She could tell he was trying hard not to yell into the phone.

"How did this happen? There's a night shift crew. Why didn't they call us?"

"They were ambushed. Tied up and stuffed in the morgue fridge. I found them when I came in. They were banging on the doors to get out."

Katie squawked and covered her mouth. Her poor crew!

"Did you have security check the surveillance footage?"

"Right before I called you. Someone blacked out the cameras. No one noticed, because the lab isn't actively monitored. It's a passive system."

Alex muttered a curse. "Is the sheriff aware?"

"He and Deputy Travers are here now. The sheriff called in the FBI. We're waiting on their CSI team to arrive and process the scene."

"Okay. We'll be there as soon as we can," Katie said. "Cooperate with the feds when they arrive."

"You got it, boss."

Devin hung up, and Alex closed the sat phone with more force than necessary. "This is getting ridiculous."

"Agreed." She slid out of the sleeping bag to get dressed. Her mind whirled. She knew they were onto something with that girl.

"What are you thinking?" Alex asked as he pulled his khaki cargo pants over his hips.

She glanced at him, her brain glitching a moment as she took in his naked chest. Looking away, she concentrated on her own nakedness and covering it up. "I'm thinking that someone is getting very nervous. That girl's skeleton is the key, I'm telling you. But if it's been smashed along with the others, it could take weeks for investigators to sort out the pieces."

"I wonder if they got to the large evidence storage. You put her clothes back there, didn't you?"

Her face brightened. "I did." She pulled her t-shirt over her head and held out a hand. "Give me the phone."

Alex passed her the device. She flipped it open and dialed Devin back.

"Hello?"

"Devin, did they get to large evidence storage?"

There was a brief pause. "I'm not sure. I didn't think to check. Let me go up there, and I'll call you back."

She folded the phone closed as he hung up. "He's checking. Let's get this camp broken down and get out of here."

With quick, efficient movements, they finished dressing and rolled up the sleeping bags they'd zipped together. They were dismantling the tent when the sat phone rang again.

Alex was closest and answered it, putting it on speaker again.

"It's still there. I let the sheriff know, and he posted a deputy on the door."

Yes!

"Awesome. Thanks, Dev."

"Yep. See you soon."

Alex hung up. "Finally! I hope the key to this thing is in her clothes."

"Me too, but I'm not holding my breath." But if it was there, she was going to find it, FBI taking over be damned.

EIGHT

Reeves was pacing in front of Alex's SUV when they entered the parking lot.

"It's about time. Sheriff Archer's been calling me every five minutes. I keep telling him you're on the way, but he's still ready to have my ass in a sling. Throw your stuff in the back so we can go."

Alex eyed the young deputy with a frown, but did as he asked. Katie opened the back door to get in, but Alex walked up to Reeves and held out a hand. "Give me the keys."

"What? No. You're in protective custody. I'm driving."

"Not this time, you're not. I'm keyed up, and I already hate having someone else drive me. And it's my car. Give me the keys."

The deputy eyed him, ready to protest again.

"Just do it, Austin," Katie said. "He'll just stand there until you do."

Reeves pressed his lips together, his jaw working, but he slapped the keys into Alex's outstretched hand.

"Thanks. If Seb yells at you, tell him I took the keys and

got in the driver's seat and refused to move." Alex opened the driver's door and climbed in.

Katie got in the back, smiling. "I'll vouch for you. He actually did that to me."

The deputy rolled his eyes and buckled his seatbelt. "Thanks. Just do me a favor and keep it at the speed limit, yeah? Nothing's going to change in the extra couple of minutes it'll take us to get there."

Alex nodded and started the car, pulling out of the lot.

Katie settled back into the seat, her mind going over what they knew about the body. She wished she'd had a chance to run the bone sample she prepped. Her hope had been to run the mineral content against tap water data and see if she could come up with a town or city—hell, even a region would suffice —where the girl grew up. It could help narrow down the search.

The pop of a tire jolted her from her thoughts. The car lurched and swung wildly until Alex got it under control. He slowed and pulled onto the shoulder, putting the vehicle in park. "Call Seb and tell him we ran into a delay," he said to Reeves.

The young deputy nodded, already reaching for his radio.

Katie climbed out to help Alex with the tire, crouching down to inspect it while he opened the back hatch to get the jack. She found the hole and frowned as she got a closer look. That looked like a bullet hole.

She rocked back on her heels and glanced around, unease creeping up her spine. They were sitting ducks out here.

The sound of an engine reached her a moment before a black SUV came flying around the curve, skidding to a halt behind them. A man holding a pistol stepped out. Reeves moved to draw his gun, and the man shot him before the deputy could clear his weapon from his holster.

Katie shrieked and held up her hands, taking several steps

back. Blood bloomed on Reeves's shoulder, but he stayed on his feet.

"Remove your weapon, deputy, and place it on the ground."

Reeves complied, wincing as he bent down.

"Kick it away."

He kicked it into the grass.

"Now, all three of you are going to come with me." He motioned them forward with his gun.

Katie looked at Alex, tears blurring her vision. She didn't want to get in that SUV.

"Move!" the man barked. "Or I shoot the cop again."

The dead serious glint to the man's eyes told her he meant what he said. She inched forward, reaching for Alex's hand as they neared the other car. He threaded his fingers through hers, tucking her close to his body as they made their way to the vehicle.

"That's close enough."

They stopped.

"Deputy, take your handcuffs and cuff yourself."

Wincing again, Reeves reached behind his back and took out his cuffs, locking them around his wrists.

The man took a few steps back and reached through the open window of his car to withdraw two sets of zip cuffs. Katie's stomach fell as she realized these were the reinforced kind and not the simple zip ties Rayna Nydert busted out of a few weeks ago.

"Ms. Mitchum, come take these."

Her eyes widened as he used her name, but she stepped forward and took the cuffs.

"Do your boyfriend first."

She walked up to Alex and held out the cuffs, the tears spilling over now.

"It's okay," he whispered, holding up his hands.

She slid the plastic over them and pulled the ends to tighten the cuffs.

"Good," the man said. "Put your own on. Use your teeth to tighten them."

Katie did as he said, then held up her bound hands.

He motioned them to the car. "You two in the backseat. Deputy, you get to ride in the cargo area." He backed up as they moved forward, waiting for Alex and Katie to get in before opening the hatch for Reeves. Once they were all settled, he got in the driver's seat.

"Don't try anything," he warned, looking at them through the rearview mirror.

Katie huddled closer to Alex and tried to keep it together. Falling apart wouldn't help. Instead, she stared out the window and did her best to memorize the route. It bothered her a bit that he hadn't blindfolded them or worn a mask. And why he hadn't just killed them, she didn't know. Something changed, but she had no clue what. Whoever hired this man must think they knew something or had something. Once he realized they had nothing, it wouldn't end well. But she would lie through her teeth if she had to. They just needed time to formulate an escape plan.

She wasn't about to die because someone wanted to protect their sick self.

The miles ticked by while Alex seethed. If he didn't think they'd crash, he'd wrap his bound hands around the asshole's neck. He also wanted to know who was behind this. Someone was determined to keep the truth hidden, and he wanted to know why.

He sat straighter, taking in everything when the man turned onto a gravel drive that split through the trees. They were well into the mountains now, and while they'd risen in elevation, they hadn't passed the tree line. The forest here was dense.

A large cabin came into view. It would be idyllic if not for the circumstances. Smoke rose from the chimney and rocking chairs sat on the porch that ran the length of the cabin. Another dark SUV was parked next to the structure.

Their kidnapper pulled up next to the other car and parked. He glanced back at them. "Get out." Not waiting for them to comply, he opened his door and climbed out.

Alex and Katie shared a look before following. They met at the back of the vehicle, where the man let Reeves out. The deputy groaned as he rolled out of the SUV. Alex ran an assessing eye over the young man. Blood soaked the right sleeve of his shirt. Sweat dotted his forehead and his skin was pale. The kid needed fluids and medical attention. Alex was surprised he could stand.

"You need to let me tend to the deputy's wound."

"Why? It'll just be a waste of supplies. Once Pressley's done with you, none of you will have need of medical attention."

Shock made his stomach roll. He hadn't wanted to believe it, but he could no longer deny Amanda was behind all their troubles. She must have staged her abduction to throw suspicion elsewhere.

The man waved them toward the cabin with the gun in his hand. "Inside."

They filed ahead of him and up the porch stairs. Alex twisted the doorknob with his bound hands, letting it swing inward.

"Come in, Dr. Randall."

Alex frowned as it was a male voice speaking. He'd expected Amanda's.

"Move."

He stiffened at the kidnapper's command but stepped over the threshold. The first thing he noticed was the man standing behind a leather easy chair. Movement drew his eyes to his right. He saw Amanda sitting on the couch, wringing her hands in her lap as she watched them enter.

"You've got a lot of fucking nerve." He took three rapid steps toward her, but the man behind the chair drew a gun and pointed it at him. Alex stopped and glared at them both.

"That's quite enough, Dr. Randall. Have a seat next to my daughter, please."

Alex's eyes widened, and he glanced at Katie, who looked equally stunned.

"Mandy?"

Her face crumpled, and she closed her eyes as tears spilled over. "Please, just sit," she whispered.

With another glance at Katie, they sat down next to her, Katie on the end and Alex sandwiched between. Deputy Reeves sank into a side chair, looking more peaked than before.

"What's going on?" Katie asked. "Who are you, and why have you been trying to kill us? And speaking of, why *aren't* we dead? Why kidnap us this time?"

"My name is David Pressley. I'm Amanda's father, much to her dismay."

Alex looked at Mandy. Tears silently tracked down her cheeks, but she stared at the man, hatred spewing from her eyes.

He turned back to Pressley. "Okay. What does that have to do with anything?"

"Amanda, dear, why don't you explain?"

"Don't call me that, you rotten bastard," she ground out through clenched teeth.

Pressley rolled his eyes. "Just tell the damn story."

"Fine." She took a deep breath. "I lied to you when you

asked me what was so special about that girl. She reminded me of someone. When I was young, my best friend had a younger sister, Tanya. She disappeared when Kim and I were in college."

"What does your dad have to do with her disappearance? What's his connection to the Paulsons?" Alex asked.

"Mom divorced him when I was young. I didn't find out until I was older, but he liked underage prostitutes. When she found out about it, she left him."

"Did he—" Katie broke off, eyes wide.

Amanda shook her head, catching her meaning. "No. He never touched me. I guess he drew the line somewhere." She cast a derisive glance at her father before continuing. "When we pulled up that girl, something about her bugged me. I couldn't put my finger on it until we were on the way back. Then, I realized it was her clothes. They looked like the same ones Tanya had on when she disappeared. The more I looked at her, the more I was sure. What I didn't know until the other day is that the Paulsons snatched her from the movie theater where she worked. Seems he," she nodded at her father, "liked their service. From what he said, Tanya freaked when she saw him. He claims he just gave her enough drugs to calm her down."

Alex turned to Pressley. "So, how did she die, then?"

"She had a reaction to the drugs," he said. "Anaphylaxis."

"To opioids? You expect us to believe that? Do you know how rare an allergy that is?" Katie said.

"Believe me, don't believe me. I don't care. It's the truth." He walked around the chair to perch on the edge. Clasping his hands, he rested his elbows on his knees, leaning forward. "When I learned the Paulsons were in custody and then what you unearthed, I went into damage control mode. I took Amanda from the hospital parking lot to find out what she knew. My—associate—panicked when the two of you came out. Amanda saw you and yelled. You must not have heard her, but it didn't matter. Tony shot at you, hoping to eliminate you as witnesses." He glared at the man standing sentry by the door. "All he did was create more headaches for me. He tried to clean up his mess, but failed at that too, so I told him to bring the two of you to me and I'd fix it."

He stood. "I can't let it get out that I'm involved. It'll ruin my career—everything I've built will go up in smoke. I've done a lot of good, and all of it will be questioned. Terrible people could go free."

"Wait." Katie held out a hand. "What do you mean? Are you an attorney?"

"He's a judge," Amanda said, her eyes hard. "A federal judge."

Alex snorted. "That makes sense. Brandt was a judge too. How many more of your buddies are involved? And how did you know what we found?"

Pressley's eyes widened a fraction as he realized he'd let something slip he shouldn't have. His expression quickly cleared, though. "None of that matters. You'll all be dead in the next few hours—well, at least you, Ms. Mitchum, and this poor deputy. My daughter will have a choice."

"So, why not tell us, then?" Katie said. "Give us some closure before you condemn us to death."

Pressley grinned and touched his temple. "You're a quick one, but I'm not stupid. Even a foolproof plan can go off the rails under the right set of circumstances."

Alex frowned. What the hell was he talking about? Why didn't he just shoot them and get it over with?

Pressley looked at Tony. "Do you have everything you need for their disposal?"

Tony nodded.

"Good. Do it. I'm going to have a chat with my daughter

and make our final arrangements. Don't screw it up, or you're joining them. Understand?"

Tony's jaw twitched, but he nodded and walked closer. "Up." He pushed on Reeves's shoulder. The deputy moaned and staggered to his feet. "You too." He pointed at Alex and Katie.

"Dad. Dad, you can't. Please," Amanda begged, rising with them.

"Hush, girl. Do you think your career won't be affected if it comes out your father played a role in those girls' deaths? I'm doing this for you too."

"Bullshit! It's only ever been about you."

He narrowed his eyes at her. "You're not going to stay quiet if I let you live, are you?"

"Fuck no!"

He held her gaze a moment before taking a deep breath and squaring his shoulders. "Very well. It seems you'll meet the same fate as your friends. I'm sorry, my dear."

Alex felt a surge of pride for his friend as she faced her father. It couldn't be easy to know her own flesh and blood was willing to sacrifice her to save his reputation.

"If you were, you'd turn yourself in. I hope you rot in hell."

"Yes, well, I see you take after your mother. Tony, get them out of here."

Tony gave Reeves a shove. The man crashed into Amanda, who caught him around the waist and helped him to the back door. Alex and Katie followed, with Tony at their back.

Outside, a white work van sat at the bottom of the steps.

"Inside."

"You're a man of few words, aren't you?" Alex said. His eyes scanned their surroundings, looking for anything to help him overpower their captor. But there was nothing.

Amanda opened the van door and Reeves fell inside. She

got in next to him and helped him sit, then Alex and Katie climbed in.

"What do we do?" Katie whispered as soon as the door closed.

"There's a knife," Reeves panted. "In my boot." He swallowed hard. "Dumbass didn't search me."

Alex shifted so his back blocked Tony's view of them. Amanda kept one eye on their driver as he got into the van and started the engine, and the other on locating and removing Reeves's knife.

They bumped over the uneven ground as Tony drove them deeper into the woods. The ride was too jarring to try to cut themselves free. They'd have to make a move once they stopped. He motioned for Mandy to hide it in her clothes. She still had on her scrubs from the day she disappeared, so she tucked it into the front pocket.

He clenched his teeth, knowing they had to mount some kind of offense or they were going to die. The van just needed to stop so they could.

After another five minutes—and several bone-jarring bumps—they came to a halt. Tony exited the vehicle, and Alex shifted, ready to climb out.

"If you get a chance to use that knife, take it," he whispered.

Amanda nodded.

The doors opened, and they squinted against the light.

"Out." Tony stood there, a gun trained on them and a black duffel slung over his shoulder.

Katie was closest to the door and got out first. Tony grabbed her and thrust his pistol into her side. Alex's heart stuttered.

Amanda followed Katie out, then turned to help Reeves. Alex pushed him from behind the best he could with his hands bound. The deputy's pallor had worsened and there was an ominous rattle to his breathing that Alex didn't like. If they didn't get the man help soon, he was going to die.

They got him upright, but he couldn't stand on his own. Amanda was the only one whose hands weren't bound, so the task of hauling him around fell to her, but she was a foot shorter and eighty pounds lighter than the young man.

"Help her," Tony growled, looking at Alex.

Alex held up his hands. "How?"

The other man grunted and withdrew a knife from his pocket. Flicking it open, he cut through Alex's bonds, then put the gun back in Katie's side.

"You try anything, she dies."

Katie's wide eyes stared at him with fear. Alex made a small nod, then took Reeves's weight from Amanda.

"Move," Tony said.

"Which way?" Alex growled.

"Straight."

Half supporting, half dragging Reeves, Alex walked deeper into the trees. The further they went, the harder it became for the deputy to walk. As he was about to stop and pick him up in a fireman's carry, the trees thinned out and Alex could see they were coming up to a cliff.

A few feet from the edge, the trees gave way. Tony ordered them to stop.

"Tie the deputy and Katie to a tree." He pulled a rolled rope from his bag and tossed it at Alex.

Alex hesitated, knowing they stood less of a chance of getting out of this if they were restrained.

Tony dug the gun into Katie's side. She let out a soft grunt, and her face contorted for a brief second. "Don't make me shoot her now. A shot in the gut won't kill her. Not right away."

Biting his tongue so as not to further enrage the man, he

nodded. Tony gave Katie a shove toward the tree. Alex followed her with Reeves.

"I—can't stand," Reeves breathed.

"Then sit," Alex said. He lowered the man to the ground. Katie sat next to him and Alex lashed them to the tree. Hoping Tony wasn't a knot connoisseur, he tied a quick hitch knot. With his body blocking their captor's view, he tapped Katie's arm with a finger. When she looked down, he tapped the end of the rope, then looked her in the eye. Her head bobbed a fraction, and he stood up.

Tony walked over, put a finger under the rope near Reeves's shoulder and tugged. It stayed taut. Satisfied it was secure, he pointed to the tree to his left. "Now it's your turn." He took out another rope and handed it to Amanda. "Tie him up." He pointed the gun at Katie again, knowing it would make Alex comply.

Alex clenched his teeth together, grinding away the enamel as he spun and walked to the tree. Amanda looped the rope around him and the tree trunk and tied it off.

"Last chance, sweetie," Tony said to Amanda after he checked the rope. "You want to give daddy-dearest a pass and come back with me?"

"He'd never believe me if I did. And he'd be right not to."

Tony shrugged. "Have it your way." He raised the gun and shot her between the eyes.

Katie's shout of surprise sounded over the echo of the gun. Alex's stomach lurched and anger hit him hard in the gut as he watched Amanda fall. Using all his strength, he curled his arms, searching for the knot Amanda tied, almost sobbing in relief when he realized she tied a hitch knot as well. He yanked on the end, pushing against the rope until it slithered down to his feet.

Tony's back was to him, giving Alex a slight element of surprise. In two powerful strides, he was within reach of the other man and launched himself at him as Tony raised the gun to shoot Reeves.

The shot went wild as they fell to the ground in a tangle of limbs. Alex used his size to his advantage and stretched up to grab the wrist of Tony's gun hand, slamming it to the ground to try to make him let go. Tony bucked, sending Alex sprawling to the side, and he lost his grip. Cursing, he scrabbled to flip over, turning in time to see Tony stagger to his feet and aim the gun at him.

"I'm going to enjoy this. You and your lady have been a pain in my ass."

Fuck! Alex closed his eyes, knowing he lost. "I'm sorry, Katie, I tried. I love you," he whispered.

Tony grunted, and Alex's eyes popped open to see a look of surprise and pain on the man's face. He dropped to his knees, and Alex saw Katie standing behind him, holding the hilt of Reeves's knife, which stuck out of Tony's back between his fourth and fifth ribs near his spine. The gun fell from his fingers and he pitched forward, landing on his face in the dirt, the knife still stuck in his back.

~

Ohmigod, ohmigod, ohmigod! I killed a man! Katie stared at the knife sticking out of Tony's back, her stomach doing somersaults. She heard Alex get to his feet a moment before he touched her arm.

"Katie, honey? Are you all right?"

Her eyes snapped to his as she came back to herself. The words she heard him whisper as she stabbed Tony registered. She glared at him. "You picked a hell of a time to say you love me. Jerk. Having it associated with a murder and me stabbing a guy is not the way I want to remember something like that." Upset with what just occurred, she lashed out at him.

"I'm sorry, I thought I was about to die! It seemed like a good idea at the time." He cupped her face in his hands. "It doesn't change anything, though. I meant what I said. I love you. And if it helps, think of it this way—in my last moments, I professed my love for you over anything else."

She tipped her head. That was a good point. She leaned forward to rest her forehead against his chest. "I'm not really mad. Not about that. I'm sorry." She looked up. "I love you too."

Alex pressed a quick, hard kiss to her lips. "As much as I would love to savor this moment, we still have a couple problems." He looked past her. She turned to follow his gaze, her eyes hesitating on Amanda's body before landing on Reeves, who still sat propped against the tree. He was breathing, but not well. *God, what a mess!*

She looked back at Alex. "We need to take care of Amanda's dad, too."

Alex's eyes hardened, flickering to his friend lying on the ground. "Yeah. Let's load Reeves in the van and go find the bastard." He bent down and rummaged in Tony's pocket, locating his knife, then using it to cut Katie's wrists apart.

"Thank you." She rubbed her wrists.

"Check his pockets for a phone. And get the car keys and his gun." Alex walked over to Reeves.

Katie looked down at Tony's still form and wrinkled her nose before crouching down next to him. Thankfully, she could see the outline of a cell in his back pocket. She slid her fingers just inside the edge and plucked it out.

"Found it!" Turning it on, she touched the emergency call button, but it showed no service.

Because, of course, we're in the boonies. She tucked the phone into her pocket with a sigh of disgust, then rolled Tony enough to reach into his front pants pocket for the keys. Trying not to think about what she was doing, she wiggled her hand into his pocket. Her fingers hit the key ring, and she hooked it, pulling it free. Picking up the gun that laid on the ground by his hand, she pushed to her feet, then hurried over to see if Alex needed help.

"No signal?" he asked, looking up at her from his position crouched next to Reeves.

She shook her head, frowning. "Nope. Maybe there will be one closer to the cabin."

"Let's hope so. I don't know how much longer he's going to hang on. He's unconscious now." He looped Reeves's arm over his shoulder and snagged his leg, then stood, muscles flexing and bulging with the effort of deadlifting the two-hundred-pound deputy. With a quick readjustment to better distribute Reeves's weight, he started toward the van at a fast walk.

Even carrying the man and knowing where they were going, it still took them nearly ten minutes to walk through the forest. By the time they reached the car, sweat dripped off Alex's brow in rivulets. When the car came into sight, Katie ran ahead and opened the back doors for him, then helped get Reeves settled. Once the deputy was as comfortable as they could get him, she ran around toward the passenger seat.

"You drive," Alex said.

She paused. "Are you sure?"

He nodded. "I need a minute."

She stared at him a moment longer, then ran around the front of the van and hopped into the driver's seat. Thrusting the key into the ignition, she started the vehicle and put it into drive as Alex closed the door.

Katie drove as fast as she dared over the rough terrain. She hit a bump that threw them forward so hard, she was surprised she didn't get whiplash. Or break an axle on the van.

"What's the plan?" she asked, not taking her eyes off the ground ahead of them.

"Not sure." Alex braced a hand against the dash, trying not to bounce out of his seat.

She hit another nasty pothole, and they heard Reeves groan from the back.

"Sorry," she whispered. At least they knew he was still alive, though.

"Damn, this car is not built for this terrain."

No, it was not. She really should slow down, but time wasn't on their side.

"We can't go into this with no plan. I mean, I know I usually fly by the seat of my pants, but in this case, it feels wrong. So, what's our plan? Why don't you have a plan? You always have a plan." Her voice rose with each question until she was a couple octaves above her normal range. Tears pressed behind her eyes, and she blinked furiously to keep them away.

Alex touched her leg, his touch grounding her.

"Take a breath, honey. We'll figure it out. Everything hinges on where Pressley is when we arrive. I don't want to have to sneak inside to get to him, so if he isn't outside, we need to lure him there."

Katie's mind cleared at his gentle, no-nonsense tone, before filling with ways to lure Pressley out. She pointed at the glove box. "Open that and tell me what's in there."

He pulled the latch and rummaged through it. "What am I looking for?"

"Stuff."

He paused and glanced at her. She rolled a hand. "I'll know it when I see it. What's in there?"

"Um, fast-food napkins, car manuals, and a tire gauge."

"Okay. How about in here?" She pointed to the console between them.

Alex flipped open the top. "More napkins, pens, candy," she heard rattling as he poked through the compartment, "and a lighter."

"Ha!" Her tone was triumphant. "The lighter. And all the napkins."

"I'm afraid to ask, but why do you need a lighter?"

She grinned, correcting their course as they went over another nasty bump. "I'm going to turn this van into a bomb."

Alex's eyes widened before closing as he shook his head. "Of course you are," he muttered. "Just don't kill us."

Was he for real? "You know I play with chemicals all day, every day, right?"

He rolled his eyes. "So you have a plan, then?"

"Yes. I'm going to stop at the tree line. We'll get Austin out of the back, then I'll drive up to the house and light the gas tank on fire."

"Wait. No. How about you stay with Reeves and I'll light the van up?"

She shook her head. "That won't work. I can't carry him. While I drive the van up to the house, you need to work your way around to the front of the house with him, so we can be ready to get out of here."

"Okay, but what happens when Pressley comes outside when the van blows and sees you?"

"We have Tony's gun." She looked at him. "And Austin's handcuffs. I'll hold him at gunpoint until you make it to the house and can cuff him."

He arched a brow. "Just like that? What happens if he resists?"

Katie shrugged. "Then I shoot him. Not to kill, though. That bastard needs to stand trial for what he's done and rot in jail the rest of his miserable life."

Alex turned in his seat to stare at her. "I'm not sure I like this plan. It puts you in too much danger."

"I'll be fine. I know how to handle a weapon."

"I know you do, but that's not what I'm worried about.

There's a myriad of things that could go wrong. Leaving you to face all of that alone—it scrapes against the grain, Katie."

"Well, do you have a better plan?"

The corners of his eyes crinkled as he thought. She could practically hear the gears turning as he tried to come up with an alternative. But the fact Reeves couldn't walk put a damper on what they could do. She couldn't carry the deputy, which meant capturing Pressley fell to her.

"Dammit," he muttered, coming to the same conclusion she had. "Fine."

"Good. I'm glad you agree, because it's time to implement this plan." She pulled the van to a halt just before they broke through the trees to the yard around the cabin. Smoke no longer rose from the chimney. It looked like Pressley was ready to move on.

Katie put the van in park and climbed out to help Alex get Reeves out of the vehicle. She opened the doors, then hopped inside to lift the young man's head and shoulders to slide him forward. His skin had a ghostly pallor to it now, and he was clammy to the touch. They needed to hurry.

As Alex lifted Reeves onto his shoulders, the deputy groaned. His eyes opened to slits before fluttering closed again.

"Make it quick, babe."

She nodded, closing the van doors with a soft click. "Be careful." She stretched up and pecked him on the cheek.

"You too."

"I will."

Turning, she ran around to the driver's side and got in. She grabbed all the napkins and twisted them into a thick rope so she wouldn't have to take time once she was in sight of the cabin's windows, then put the van in gear and bumped over the grass to park out front.

Eyes on the cabin's door and windows, she slipped out of the van, napkin rope and lighter in her hands. At the rear of the vehicle, she twisted off the gas cap and stuffed the makeshift wick into the gas tank, leaving several inches hanging out.

"Here goes nothing," she whispered to herself. She lit the lighter and touched the flame to the end of the napkins. As soon as it caught, she took off running, hiding behind one of the parked SUVs.

Peering over the hood of the car, she waited. "Come on, come on, come on. Blow, dammit!" Flames licked the side of the van now as the gasoline caught.

The fire flickered, then a small ball of flames whooshed out of the tank just before it exploded. She ducked and covered her head, waiting several moments before peering around the car again. The cabin door opened, and Pressley rushed out, his gun in his hand. He paused at the edge of the porch, glancing around. She knew she had to move now, or she'd lose her chance.

Katie ran around the side of the car and raised the pistol in her hands. "Pressley! Drop the gun and put your hands up!"

The man whirled in her direction, his eyes going wide as he saw her standing there aiming a gun at him. When his gun arm moved as he took aim at her, she fired one shot in his direction, deliberately missing him. He froze.

"That was a warning. The next one won't miss. Drop it."

He bared his teeth, cursing, but let the gun drop from his hand.

"Kick it off the porch."

His foot swept it onto the grass below. "Dammit. I knew I should have just killed you all myself. How did you get away?"

"He made us tie ourselves up, then didn't check the knots. Hitch knots look complicated and secure, but they come apart with one tug. Why did you hire such an inept contract killer, anyway?"

"He came recommended."

She arched a brow. "By whom?"

Realizing he'd already said too much, he pressed his lips together.

"Fine. Don't talk. I'm sure it'll all come out in court."

Movement from her side caught her attention. Alex emerged from the trees. He ran past her and up the porch steps to handcuff Pressley.

"Ow! That's too tight." Pressley stood on his toes as Alex closed the cuffs.

Katie heard one more click.

"Yeah? Well, your daughter can't feel anything ever again. Tony killed her. Deal with it." He yanked on Pressley's arm, hauling him down the stairs.

Lowering the gun, Katie opened the back hatch on Tony's SUV. Alex put him inside.

"Watch him. I'm going to go get Reeves."

She nodded, and he jogged off. Pressley sat against the window, his knees drawn up and his head bent. He stayed that way even as Alex walked up with the deputy over his shoulders.

Katie shut the hatch, then opened the back passenger door and climbed in. Alex lowered Reeves to the seat, and she helped pull him across. Blood still oozed from his shoulder, and his breathing rattled. She fished in her pocket for the car keys.

"Here." She threw them at Alex. "Drive."

He caught them with a deft hand and didn't hesitate to climb into the driver's seat.

"You still got that phone?" he asked as they shot down the gravel driveway to the highway.

She took it from her back pocket, keeping an eye on Pressley, who still sat staring at his knees. Turning on the screen, she cursed. "It still says no service."

Alex turned onto the highway and gunned the engine. "Keep checking."

"Duh." She stared at the screen, willing a bar to pop up. Alex rounded a sharp bend, and the road opened to the valley below. Two bars popped up on the screen. Heart leaping into her throat, she pushed the emergency call button, then send to connect with nine-one-one.

"Boone County emergency services. Please state the nature of your emergency."

"This is Katie Mitchum with forensics. I'm with the medical examiner, Dr. Alex Randall. We're heading into town with Deputy Reeves. He's been shot. We'll be pulling up to the hospital ER in about ten minutes. We also have the man who shot him. He's uninjured and in cuffs. Can you have the sheriff meet us there?"

The dispatcher cleared his throat. "Um, yes. Okay. Is there any other information you'd like me to pass along to the hospital staff?"

"Tell them Reeves is in shock and he's lost a significant amount of blood."

"Yes, ma'am. Drive safe."

"We will, thank you." She hung up. "They're expecting us, and Seb will meet us there." She put the phone away, then bent her head to check on Reeves. "We're almost at the hospital, Austin. Hang on." His breathing was growing raspier by the minute. She checked his pulse and found it weak.

Glancing up, she willed the car to go faster—much faster —and said a prayer.

∼

A cup of coffee appeared under Alex's nose. He glanced up to see Seb standing over him.

"Thanks." He accepted the cup and took a sip. The sheriff

handed another cup to Katie, then sat down across from them.

"So, you guys want to tell me what happened? We found your car on the highway. I take it they set a trap?"

Alex nodded. "Yeah. Someone shot out the tire—probably Pressley—or it could have been Tony, his hitman. He showed up about a minute after the tire blew. He shot Reeves, then forced us all into his car. Pressley was waiting for us at the cabin. He told Tony to take us into the woods and dispose of us. I don't know how that guy managed to commit so many murders. He bungled every attempt at getting rid of us."

"Did Pressley tell you why he did all this?"

Katie nodded. "The Jane Doe Amanda was so enamored with was the younger sister of one of her friends. The Paulsons kidnapped her, and Pressley was one of their customers."

Seb let out a low whistle. "I didn't know about the friend part. We did find out that Pressley was one of the ring's clients, though. Brandt finally talked. Seems he got a taste of what it's like to be a former judge in the jail's general population. He traded some information—and the password to an encrypted thumb drive he had—for a more solitary existence. We found Pressley's name on it."

"So, he was screwed either way." Alex winced. "I just wish we knew all that before he kidnapped Amanda to find out what she knew."

"Me too."

"Are Jackie and her team on the way up to the cabin to retrieve her body and Tony's?" Katie asked.

Seb shook his head. "The feds are handling that. I'd already turned the case over to them, so they're taking care of processing the scene. They also arrested Amos White."

Alex's eyes grew huge. "What? Why?"

"They found his name on the thumb drive as well, and he confessed to being friends with Amanda's father. He says he only went a handful of times years ago, but it was enough for Pressley to blackmail him with. He's the one who told Pressley what you two found."

"Oh my God. Is there anyone in a position of authority *not* involved?" Katie asked.

"Right?" Seb shook his head. "It's an extensive list, and the repercussions are going to be severe. But, we—you—have brought down a significant operation and given a lot of families closure." He paused and studied them for a moment. "I have to say, I'm impressed. You two make a damn good team."

Katie glanced at Alex, a soft smile on her face. "I guess we do."

He smiled back. "Yeah. We do."

Seb grinned. "Just don't make a habit of taking out the bad guys for me. Stick to forensics and let me and my deputies handle them?"

"Trust me, we will," Alex said. "Speaking of deputies, have you heard an update on Reeves?"

"I just talked to the doctor, actually. He's not out of the woods yet, but the doctor is optimistic. He's got a long recovery ahead of him, though. The bullet broke bones and damaged the radial nerve. It may be a while before he regains full function."

"Well, if there's anything we can do, let us know," Katie said.

"I will. After you talk to the feds, go home and get some rest."

They nodded.

"I'll see you later." He waved and left.

Alex slumped in his seat, exhausted. Even the coffee wasn't enough to keep him alert. He glanced at Katie, who looked like he felt. But there was also relief on her face. They might still have to talk to some people, but it was over. All those children could finally rest in peace.

NINE

T*hree weeks later...*

"Is it straight?" Alex looked over his shoulder at Katie, who sat on the edge of his desk.

She tilted her head, eyeing the grouping of drawings he was attempting to hang. It wasn't quite straight. "A little more that way." She pointed to her left.

He adjusted the frame, and she nodded. Letting go, he stepped back to stand next to her, wrapping an arm around her waist. "I like the frames you picked." They were thin black metal, which set the drawings off from the wall just enough.

"Good. I was afraid you'd think they were too plain, but I didn't want to overshadow your artwork."

She smiled up at him, still unable to believe the turn her relationship with this man had taken. A few weeks ago, she wouldn't have cared if he had any interest in her opinion. Now his opinion mattered more than any other's. And she loved it.

She loved *him*. It was still difficult to wrap her head around that. And that he loved her back.

"They look great. Now, if we could just work on the rest of your office." She looked around at the boringness that was Alex's office. Beige met her eyes everywhere she looked.

He frowned. "What's wrong with my office?"

"It looks like someone took an eraser to it and removed all the color."

He laughed. "I guess it does, but I've never really cared too much about what my office looks like. It's just a workspace."

"Yeah, but it should be someplace you like spending time in, since you're here so much."

Alex shrugged. "Maybe you should just spend more time in here. You brighten the space up considerably." His eyes turned a midnight blue as he stared down at her.

Katie blushed and cleared her throat. "Yes, well, I don't think the staff would like that very much. Maybe we should just stick to adding some throw pillows or some plants."

Another laugh broke free of his chest. He leaned down and pressed a kiss to her cheek. "I'll work on that. But how about we get out of here for now?"

With a grin, she hopped off the desk. "Yes. We should get going, or we're going to be late." Tomorrow was Jace and Tara's wedding, and they were both in it. Tonight was the rehearsal dinner.

Alex picked up his coat and shrugged into it. "Did you remember to grab the wine?"

Katie nodded, leading the way out of his office. He closed and locked the door behind them before they made their way to her desk, where she donned her coat and retrieved her purse from the desk drawer.

"I ran out at lunch to get it. I can't believe the wine they ordered for the dinner was stolen. Why would someone do that?"

"Probably someone looking to make a quick buck. But I don't mind it being a bring your own wine party. Makes for an interesting evening." He grinned down at her, his hand going to the small of her back as they walked out of the lab and onto the elevator.

The doors closed, and Katie swayed into him. "You know what makes for an even more interesting evening?"

His pupils dilated as he stared down at her. "What?"

"The lingerie I bought to wear with my bridesmaid's dress. You're going to love it."

He wrapped an arm around her waist. "Dammit, woman. And you're going to make me wait until tomorrow night to see it, aren't you?"

She cackled. "Yep."

He growled, then raised an eyebrow. "Well, maybe I'll make you wait to see the surprise I have for you in the car."

Katie straightened. Surprise? She hadn't noticed anything when they came to work this morning or when she went to the store at lunch to get the wine for tonight. "What are you talking about?"

The elevator dinged and the doors opened. He waggled his brows, then let her go and stepped off.

"Alex." Her voice held a warning note.

He just smiled and kept walking.

Sometimes, she hated him as much as she loved him. Why did he have to tease her so?

They left the hospital and walked to the doctor's lot. Once in the car, she pounced.

"Where is it?" She opened the glove box and started poking through.

He laughed and laid a hand over hers. "It's not in there, love." Reaching up, he flipped down his visor and a set of papers fell out.

"I about had a heart attack when you went to the store. I was so afraid you'd find these."

"What are they?"

He handed them to her.

She unfolded the papers and frowned. "Plane tickets? To Hawaii?" She looked up, a curious frown on her face.

"I figured after the last several months, we were due a vacation. The powers that be agreed with me. We'll be spending Thanksgiving soaking up the sun in beautiful Waikiki."

Her frown morphed into a bright smile. "Yes!" She flung her arms around his neck and kissed him. "This is exactly what I needed. Can we take our climbing equipment too? They do have mountains."

He grinned. "I was already planning on it." His face sobered, and he brushed a lock of her hair away from her face, then traced the line of her cheekbone to her nose and down over her lips.

A slow burn erupted in Katie's belly. Oh, what this man could do to her with just a touch.

"I love you. So much."

Katie leaned in and pressed a fierce kiss to his mouth, then pulled back to look in his eyes. "I love you too. We need to celebrate later. I might be persuaded to model my swimsuits for you." She frowned. "If I can find them." The day after their encounter with Pressley, Alex asked her to move in with him. She hadn't hesitated and hastily packed her small house. But that meant lots of unlabeled boxes.

He laughed. "I'll help you look for them." With the push of a button, he started the car's engine. "I'm thinking you might not need them as much as you'd think, though." Heat radiated from his eyes as he glanced at her.

Katie shivered. "Yeah?" She toyed with the hair at his nape with one finger. He growled.

"Yeah. And if you don't stop that, we're not going to make

it out of the garage once we get home and then we'll be really late to the rehearsal."

She grinned. "Hmm... It's been a long time since I had sex in a car."

"Jesus, Katie, you're killing me."

She giggled and sat back. "Good. Payback for all the years I had to watch you strut around the office in scrubs and a lab coat."

His smile was wicked. "I have one at home. Do you need a doctor?"

"Desperately." She laughed, loving the freedom that came with their relationship. Ruffling his feathers now led to great fun rather than a load of frustration, sexual and otherwise. She shifted in her seat and left him alone so he could get them home safely. She didn't want anything to derail their plans.

"I have one more surprise waiting. It was delivered today while we were at work," he said, turning onto the main road.

She turned in her seat, curious. "What is it?"

He waggled a finger at her. "Oh, no. I'm not telling you anything. You're just going to have to be patient."

Katie huffed and crossed her arms, making him laugh.

"You look like a pissed off kitten."

"Cats have claws, remember." Her angry meow and hiss filled the interior of the car.

"Down, kitty. We'll be there soon enough."

Rolling her eyes, she laughed at herself and sat back. Her brain whirled as she tried to figure out what he could have bought, but nothing came to mind. Resigning herself to wait-ing, she settled back into her seat and enjoyed the short drive home. After several minutes, he pulled into the driveway and parked the car in the garage. She was out of the SUV in a flash, running out of the garage to the porch for the package she saw when they drove up.

"Slow down. It's not going to walk away."

She crouched in front of the box and glanced up at him, grinning. "Shiny."

He laughed and crouched next to her as she ripped the tape off and opened the box. Rummaging through the packing material, she unearthed two garden gnomes. A giggle spilled free, and she sank onto her butt as waves of laughter rolled out. The gnomes were exactly like the ones she described to him that night Tony broke into the house and tried to shoot them.

Alex took them out of the box, chuckling with her as she continued to laugh. "What do you think?"

She swiped at the tears rolling down her cheeks, her laughter subsiding to soft giggles. "I think they're perfect." She picked up the one dressed in tie-dye and stood. "Let's find them a place out front."

He picked up the one in plaid and suspenders and followed her off the porch. She stared at the landscaping a moment before walking toward the bushes in front of the living room windows. They set them down, then stepped back to admire their new decorations.

Katie giggled again. "Those are fantastic." She stretched up onto her toes and pressed a kiss to Alex's lips. "Thank you."

He smiled down at her and gave her a quick kiss. "I know you've been here a few weeks already, but now it really feels like the house belongs to both of us. Welcome home, Katie."

Smiling ear-to-ear, she tugged him toward the house. "Come on. Let's go find my swimsuits."

Heat darkened his eyes. "I wish we had more time. But I think you should forget the swimsuits. I'll rebook us into some place with a private pool. We can just go skinny dipping."

"With a private beach too? Because I love the ocean."

He kissed her. "Yep." Sweeping her into his arms, he dashed into the garage and through the interior door.

Katie sent a silent prayer of thanks upward for this wonderful man as his mouth and hands sent her thoughts scattering to the wind.

Keep reading for a sneak peek of *Scorched*, book 5 in the *Broken Bow* series.

Thank you for reading Close Quarters! I hope you enjoyed it.

Want to read an EXCLUSIVE and FREE book? Sign up for my mailing list. You can find the sign-up form on my website, ashleyaquinn.com. My list also receives sneak peeks of my latest work and access to exclusive giveaways. Also, please consider leaving a rating or review on Amazon and or Goodreads. It would be greatly appreciated!

Thanks again for reading!
    - Ashley

~

Keep reading for a sneak peek at Book 5, Scorched in the Broken Bow series.

Scorched

BROKEN BOW
BOOK

ONE

Sweat dripped down Fire Lieutenant Declan Briggs's forehead to sting his eyes as he broke through the cloud of smoke and stepped outside. Walking to the firetruck, he set the hose down before lifting his helmet and taking off his mask. He tucked both under his arm as he inhaled a breath of smoke-scented air and swiped at the sweat on his face. A quick glance at his partner, Sam Reeves, showed him doffing his own gear.

"Hell of a fire, Lou." Declan's newest firefighter, Jameson Gehring, walked up, carrying water bottles.

Declan took the bottle held out to him and downed half of it before answering. "Yeah. It's a hot one, that's for sure. But we're winning now."

"About time. Need me to tag in?"

"No." Declan shook his head. "Keep doing what you're doing. This one is a bit wild for you yet." Jameson was a good kid, but he was very young and very green. Declan wasn't about to send him into a fire like this without more training. "Can you get me a new oxygen tank? Something is wrong with this one." The one he'd been using should have lasted twice as long, but a few minutes ago, he'd glanced down to see the oxygen level in the red. He figured it had a bad seal or valve.

With a nod, Jameson hurried to the other side of the truck to grab another tank. Declan unhooked his old one while he waited, then checked in with the other two units on scene, helping to tackle the house fire and keep it from spreading to the neighboring homes. They were making progress on the blaze, but it was slow-going. The house was fully engulfed when they arrived. It had taken one look for Declan to call in additional units.

Jameson returned with a fresh tank. Declan hooked it up, testing it before nodding to Sam. "I'm good. Let's get back in there."

Sam drew his mask down. "Let's get it."

"Make sure that tank doesn't get put with the others," Declan instructed Jameson. "It needs to be fixed."

"You got it."

Declan settled his gear into place and followed Sam back to the house. They picked up their hose and mounted the porch steps. As Sam crossed the threshold, the air around them changed. The fire sucked away from them, and Declan's eyes went wide as he realized what was happening. Before he could utter a word of warning, an explosion of heat and flames sent him flying backward through the air as the fire flashed, growing exponentially in the blink of an eye.

Pain jolted through his hip and back as he hit the ground. The air left his lungs, and he rolled to his side, gasping as he tried to draw a breath. When his lungs finally worked again, pain lanced his ribs. Groaning, he rested his head on the wet grass. His ears rang, the noises around him fading as the ringing took over.

"Lou! Lieutenant! Are you okay?"

Declan cradled his ribs, rolling to look up at Gehring, whose worried face loomed over him.

"Sir, are you okay?"

"I think so." He tried to sit up, but fire raced across his ribcage. Moaning, he clutched his side and maneuvered himself to a sitting position. "Where's Sam?"

Gehring pointed ahead of them to the left. Declan squinted, trying to bring his vision into focus, and saw Sam sprawled over the grass, not moving.

"Shit." Still clumsy from the blast, Declan got to his knees. Jameson helped him stand, and he stumbled over to Sam. Two paramedics arrived and kneeled over him to assess his injuries.

"Sam!"

One of the paramedics looked up. "Lieutenant, you shouldn't be moving around." She glanced around, presumably for another medic to take care of him.

Declan ignored her and dropped to his knees. "Sam, can you hear me?"

"He's out cold," the second paramedic said. "His pupils are equal and reactive, but a little sluggish." He wrapped a blood pressure cuff around Sam's arm. A third medic came up and squatted next to Declan.

"Lieutenant, can I take a look at you?"

Declan turned to the young man at his shoulder, Denton Truesdale. Denton's voice—and everyone else's around him—sounded as though he were shouting through a tunnel.

"You can't do anything for Sam right now. Kara and Mike have things under control. Let me assess you. The blast threw you both quite a distance."

Declan nodded reluctantly, wincing as he pushed to his feet, wobbling a bit. Denton and Jameson grabbed his arms to steady him.

"I'm fine." He shook off their grip and headed for the ambulances. Denton hurried ahead and opened the back of the one on the right. On legs shakier than Declan wanted to admit, he climbed inside and sat on the stretcher. He looked at Gehring, who stood outside, watching. "Go find Walters. Tell him he's in charge and find out where he wants you. If he has to send you into the house, you do *everything* your partner says, understand?"

Jameson nodded. "Yes, sir." He ran off to find Sergeant Walters, who headed up Ladder Three.

Feeling the blast now, Declan let his head fall back against the stretcher and closed his eyes. Everything hurt.

"I'm going to take your vitals."

"Go for it," Declan muttered.

A blood pressure cuff went around his arm and a pulse oximeter clamped over his finger. He heard some beeps as the machines got their results.

"Vitals look good, considering."

Declan opened his eyes. Denton held up a penlight.

"Follow the light."

He did as asked.

"Good. Where do you hurt? And don't say you're fine. You flew twenty feet."

A corner of Declan's mouth quirked. His people knew him well. "My ribs hurt." He pointed to the left side of his chest. "And my left hip. It took the brunt of my landing."

"Can you take off your coat so I can examine your chest?"

With a groan, he sat up. His chest was on fire. Broken ribs were just what he needed. He pulled his right arm out of his turncoat, then let the jacket slide off his left. Denton leaned forward and probed his ribcage. Declan bit back a grunt of pain as he hit a sore spot.

"You should probably get some x-rays. Just to make sure there aren't any shards or dislocated breaks lurking that could puncture your lung. I'm pretty sure you broke at least two.

There's some crepitus around the sixth lateral rib, and you're tender above and below that."

He nodded. "I'll get checked. Can I go, now?"

"So long as you promise not to go back into the fire. You need to man the radios now, sir."

Seeing as he could barely lift his arm, wrangling a firehose under pressure was most definitely out. "I'll behave." He slid off the gurney. "I'm going to check on Sam."

"I hope he's okay. After what happened to his brother, it doesn't seem right he'd get hurt badly, too."

Declan agreed. Austin was just beginning to recover after being shot in the line of duty a few weeks ago. It was touch and go for several days. He'd lost a lot of blood and infection set in. The kid spent two weeks in the hospital before he was well enough to go home. He still had a ways to go, though, before he regained full function of his arm and shoulder.

Cradling his ribs, Declan stepped out of the ambulance and went looking for Sam, finding him in the next bus. He'd come to, but looked dazed.

"How's he doing, Ericson?"

Kara Ericson, the female paramedic from earlier, glanced at him before turning her attention back to the IV line she was busy hooking up. "He'll be okay. A little concussed and some contusions, but otherwise good. You both were lucky."

"We all were." He and Sam were the only firefighters close to the house when the fire flashed. If any of them had been inside when it happened, it would be a much different situation.

"Did you get checked?" she asked.

He nodded. "Broke a couple ribs. I'm all right."

"Good. You want to ride with us to the hospital for x-rays?"

He shook his head. "No. I need to stay here and help coordinate."

She gave him a sharp look.

He held up a hand, staving off the ass-chewing. "I'll go after my shift, I swear."

"Or if you start to feel short of breath. One of those ribs could shift and puncture a lung."

"I'm aware." He reached in and patted Sam's boot. "Take care, buddy. I'll check up on you later."

Sam offered him a weak smile and nodded. Declan stepped back and closed the doors. A moment later, the ambulance pulled away. As he wandered over to Ladder Three to find Walters, he wished he'd asked Truesdale for some ibuprofen, at least. He'd have to check the firetruck. There was a bottle lurking somewhere. If not, he knew there was one in his office at the fire station.

"Walters." He walked up to the older man standing beside the ladder truck, staring up at the fire. It was still burning, the progress they made earlier erased by the blast.

"Jesus, Briggs. Are you and Reeves okay? That was some explosion. I can't believe the house is still standing."

"We're fine. Cracked ribs for me and a concussion for Reeves. He's on his way to the hospital. Do we know what caused the blast? I thought we had it contained."

"So did I. There's no word yet, though. It's too hot to get inside, but we're getting there."

Declan nodded. "Okay. Sam and I didn't make it to the back of the house before it blew, so we never checked the rooms back there."

"I'll make that the priority, then. I hope the place was unoccupied. The neighbors said it's vacant because it was a flip, but that doesn't mean there wasn't a squatter they didn't know about."

"Or a contractor working late. Okay. I'll take over here. You go coordinate an entry team."

"On it." He jogged off, and Declan sagged against the

truck. He lifted the radio mic to his mouth, pressing the talk button. "Gehring."

The radio squawked. "Sir?"

"Bring me some water, would you?"

"Yes, sir."

Declan pressed the button again, this time checking on his teams. He continued to coordinate their efforts to knock down the blaze for the next couple hours. Because of the intensity, they weren't able to get inside again until they reduced it to a smolder. The fire burned through the floor to the cellar, and they needed the visibility to walk through the house without falling through. Well aware of the danger, Declan sent Walters inside with another experienced firefighter once it was safe.

His radio crackled to life. "Briggs."

"Yeah, Walt."

"Call the coroner. We've got a body."

Declan swore, loud and long, before replying. "Copy." Switching channels, he radioed dispatch and asked them to call Dr. Randall as well as Sheriff Archer.

Dammit! Could this scene get any worse? He pushed away from the truck and went looking for the med kit. He needed that pain medicine now. His ribs weren't the only thing throbbing anymore.

"Forensics just pulled in," Gehring said, running up to Declan an hour later.

Declan lifted his head from where he rested it against the doorframe of the firetruck.

"You all right, Lou?"

"I'm fine." He hurt everywhere. The pain pills only dulled

his aches to a loud roar, but he still had a job to do. He would just have to deal. "You said forensics is here?"

The young man nodded and pointed to his left. "They're over there."

"Thanks." Declan swung his legs out the open door and lowered himself to the ground, biting back a moan as the movement shifted his broken ribs. He tucked his left arm close and walked over to the forensics van. As he got close, he could hear Dr. Randall and the chief forensic scientist Katie Mitchum arguing.

"All I'm asking for is paint, Alex."

"Of the entire room. I had to hire a crew to do it the first time because of the high ceilings."

"So, we do that again."

"What's wrong with the color it is?"

"It's—boring."

He laughed. "Not everything needs to be shades of the rainbow, love."

"I'm not asking for purple or red. A nice shade of sage would be great. I mean, if I'm going to live there, I should love it, right?"

"I thought you did love my house."

"I do. Just not the white in the living room. It's too harsh with all that natural wood."

Declan stopped in front of them at the back of the van. Alex stood on the ground, taking the things Katie handed him as they bickered. "Why are you two arguing about paint colors?"

"The walls are finally getting repaired from the shooting," Alex said.

"And I'm moving in," Katie interjected.

"She wants to paint the entire room a different color instead of just repainting the new dry wall the same color."

"Have you seen his house?" Katie asked.

Declan shook his head.

"It's all beautiful hardwoods. With white walls."

"They're eggshell," Alex countered.

She rolled her eyes at him. "Same thing. My point is, the color sucks. It's not asking much to repaint, is it?"

Declan held up his hands. "I am not getting involved in your domestic dispute. You two can work that out all on your own." There was no way she was going to get him to pick a side. He was friends and colleagues with both of them.

She huffed. "Where's a woman when you need her?"

Alex laughed and helped her out of the van. "You know I'm going to let you do whatever you want. Leave the poor man alone." He pressed a kiss to her cheek.

A pretty smile spread over her face. "Fine." She scooped her multi-colored hair into a ponytail. "So, what do we have? Dispatch said you guys found a body in the house."

"Yeah. You two have what you need?"

Alex nodded. "Lead the way."

Declan spun around and led them toward the burned-out structure. "Walters will lead you to the victim." He pointed to the man in turnout gear standing near the house, his helmet tucked under his arm as he drank a bottle of water.

"You're not going in?" Alex asked. He frowned, running an assessing gaze over Declan. "What happened? You're standing funny."

"The house flashed on us. Sam Reeves and I were too close and were thrown. I broke some ribs. Sam's at the hospital with a concussion."

"Oh my goodness!" Katie glanced up at Alex. "Who's going to take care of Austin with Sam out of commission?"

"I don't know, but I'm sure the police and fire departments will come together to make sure the brothers are properly looked after while they recover."

"Damn straight. And if they're not, I'll do it myself."

Alex patted Katie's shoulder. "Down, girl."

She huffed. "Sorry."

Declan waved her off. He knew she had a soft spot for Austin after what they went through. "Alex is right. We'll make sure they're taken care of."

"Good."

They reached Walters. "Keith will lead you to the body and help you remove it. Watch your step in there. The floor is a minefield."

Walters waved them forward. "It'll be easier if we go in through the back. The victim is in the kitchen."

Declan headed back to the truck, needing to sit. Would this call ever end?

While Alex, Katie, and Walters worked to bring the victim outside, Declan kept busy doing his best to distract himself from the ache in his chest. He raided the med kit again, this time for acetaminophen.

Another vehicle pulled up on the scene as he downed the pills. Declan watched the sheriff, Sebastian Archer, emerge from his truck. Seb spotted him and jogged over.

"Sorry it took me so long to get here. I had to go to Colorado Springs earlier. Any news yet?"

Declan shook his head. "No. They'll probably be out soon. It's been close to thirty minutes since Walters took forensics in there."

"Have you talked to the neighbors at all?"

"They said the house is vacant, so we don't know who the victim is."

"Damn. Okay. I'll go talk to them again and see if any of them remember seeing anyone hanging around lately." He took in Declan's pinched expression. "You okay? I heard about the flash over on the scanner."

"I'm fine."

Seb arched a brow. "Sure. How do you really feel?"

"Like I got blown up," he replied honestly. "I'll be okay."

"You sure? Walters can handle things. Or we can call Crichton." He mentioned the other lieutenant, Matt Crichton.

"I'm fine," he growled, his voice hard. There was no way he was going to leave and give the higher-ups another reason to doubt him. He was still recovering from being labeled a murder suspect a few months ago.

Seb held up his hands. "Okay. Do you know what caused the blaze yet?" he asked, changing the subject.

Declan shook his head. "No. We haven't been able to go in and assess the structure yet for an ignition point. It was probably electrical, though. The house was under renovation."

"Is that why it burned so hot?"

"Yeah. If there were construction materials inside, it would help fuel it."

Commotion from the side of the house drew their attention. Walters emerged, helping Dr. Randall carry a body bag. Seb and Declan walked forward, and Seb opened the back of the forensics van, climbing inside to help them stow the body.

"What can you tell me?" Seb asked as he stepped down.

Alex frowned and propped his hands on his hips. "Not much yet. It's a male. I need to get him back to the lab before I can give you anything else."

"Okay. I'll locate the owners and find out who might have had access to the house."

"And I'm going to walk through it to see if I can determine the ignition source," Declan added.

"Sounds good," Seb said. "Everyone keep me informed."

The group split up, and Declan wandered back to the firetruck to get his gear.

"Lou, what are you doing?"

Declan glanced back at Gehring after shrugging into his jacket, wincing with the movement. "My job."

"You really should stay out here and let Sergeant Walters handle things."

"Probably, but this is still my scene, and I have the most training on ignition points." Declan might be young for a lieutenant at thirty-six, but he had almost two decades of experience. He joined the Marines right out of high school, and they'd put him in a firefighting unit. The work fascinated him, and he'd taken every course the military would let him until he had high-level certifications in both hazardous materials and arson. No one was better qualified to determine the source of the fire than he.

"How about you come with me? You can be my hands." Declan picked up his helmet and gloves.

The young firefighter's face lit up. "Sure."

The two of them picked their way over the soggy grass to the back of the house.

"Watch your step. Test your footing before you put your full weight on any one point and try to step where I step."

Gehring nodded and followed Declan inside. As he did, Katie poked her head around from the garage side of the wall, a camera in her hands.

"Find anything?" Declan asked.

"Maybe. Come look at this."

He walked closer, stepping into the garage through the opening exposed by the fire.

Katie pointed at the doorjamb of the steel door. "Right there."

Declan leaned in as much as his ribs would allow and inspected the spot she indicated near the doorknob. A small piece of wood sat between the door and the frame. "Is that a wedge?" He looked up at her.

She nodded. "I think so. Someone didn't want this door to open from the inside."

He closed his eyes for a brief moment. *Shit.* "This fire wasn't an accident."

"Nope. I'd say it was also probably a deliberate homicide."

"Dammit. Okay. I'll let Seb know. Have you seen any signs of an accelerant?"

She shook her head. "Not yet, but I haven't really been looking."

"Okay." He glanced back at Gehring, who stood just inside the kitchen, wide-eyed from their conversation. "Let's go find the source of this blaze." Declan stepped back into the house, his eyes roaming the walls and floor for the telltale signs of arson. "Go get the PID from the firetruck. It's in with the field-testing equipment." The photoionization detector would give him a good idea if the arsonist used an accelerant like gasoline or something similar.

Gehring nodded and left through the back door. Declan continued his perusal of the house, noting a spot near the door where the floor was charred more than it should have been. He exited the kitchen, entering what was likely the dining room. More spots like in the kitchen darkened the floor beneath each window. He took careful steps and rounded the staircase into the living room, seeing a similar pattern. Whoever set this fire made sure every exit was obstructed. The person in the kitchen never stood a chance.

About the Author

Ashley started writing in her teens and never stopped. Her first novel, Smoky Mountain Murder, came out in 2016, and she has since published two more series and has plans for more. When not writing, you can find her with her nose stuck in a book or watching some terrible disaster movie on SyFy. An avid baseball fan, she also enjoys crafting and cooking. She lives in Ohio with her husband, two kids, three cats, and one very wild shepherd mix.

Website: https://ashleyaquinn.com

goodreads.com/ashleyaquinn

amazon.com/Ashley-A-Quinn/e/B07HCT4QST

ALSO BY ASHLEY A QUINN

Foggy Mountain Intrigue

Smoky Mountain Murder

Smoky Mountain Baby

Smoky Mountain Stalker

Smoky Mountain Doctor

Smoky Mountain K-9

Smoky Mountain Judge

The Broken Bow

A Beautiful End

Wildfire

In Plain Sight

Close Quarters

Scorched

Light of Dawn

Pine Ridge

Sweetness

Loner

Shark

Katydid

Homespun